8|97
√+

JACKALS

TOR BOOKS BY CHARLES GRANT

For Fear of the Night
In a Dark Dream
The Raven Pet
Something Stirs
Stunts
Tales from the Nightside

THE OXRUN STATION NOVELS

The Bloodwind
Dialing the Wind
The Grave
The Hour of the Oxrun Dread
The Last Call of Mourning
Nightmare Seasons
The Orchard
The Sound of Midnight

TOR BOOKS EDITED BY CHARLES GRANT

After Midnight
Midnight

THE CHRONICLES OF GREYSTONE BAY

Doom City
Greystone Bay
The SeaHarp Hotel
In the Fog

JACKALS

Charles Grant

A TOM DOHERTY ASSOCIATES BOOK
NEW YORK

This is a work of fiction. All the characters and events portrayed in this book are fictitious, and any resemblance to real people or events is purely coincidental.

JACKALS

A Forge Book
Published by Tom Doherty Associates, Inc.
175 Fifth Avenue
New York, N.Y. 10010

Library of Congress Cataloging-in-Publication Data

Grant, Charles L.
    Jackals / Charles Grant.
        p.   cm.
    "A Tom Doherty Associates Book."
    ISBN 0-312-85565-6
    1. Murderers—United States—Fiction.   I. Title.
    PS3557.R265J3   1994
    813'.54-dc20   94-32705
                                                                  CIP

First edition: October 1994

Printed in the United States of America

0   9   8   7   6   5   4   3   2   1

JACKALS

Colors mean nothing when the moon is out and a soft breeze dances with the shadows in the woods.

Sparrows get dark, and robins grow darker.

Even blood on a woman turns from bright to black.

She could see it on the backs of her hands as she walked, dried there, tightening in streaks and blotches across her skin, forming scabs, turning to stone; she flexed the left one to break the forming ragged crust, flexed the right and inhaled sharply when fire raced across the ridge of her knuckles. She clamped her palm to her thigh, pressing hard, grabbing harder, willing the pain to go away, her jaw tight, head trembling, left hand slapping the air in harsh spasms.

Until the fire died, and the blood dried, and she took a stumbling step forward and slowly collapsed to her knees.

She barely felt the night-cool blacktop as it met her, and couldn't see much beyond it because of the trees. She knew, since she had seen the country in daylight, that there were pastures and fields back there, low rounded hills with spikes of oak, stands of pine, wood fences, stone fences, barbed-wire fences to keep cows and horses from wandering off the grass. She thought she remembered a small, heart-shaped pond with reeds and cattails along one bank.

She couldn't see it now.

The late August moon was bright, nearly full, washing the sky with dull silver, but the trees were tight with shadows that danced, and all she could really see was the dark stretch of road ahead, the dark of it behind where it ducked around a curve, curved again, and crossed a creek.

Her head bowed wearily between her rigid arms; she took a breath that hurt her lungs, and another that shuddered when her ribs protested, and she looked up through dark hair that dangled wetly over her eyes. The road topped a low rise long after the trees had fallen away. A house on the other side, she knew it was there. A small place. No luxuries. She didn't care. She wanted a roof above her.

She wanted to bury the goddamned moon.

Vision blurred suddenly, and suddenly snapped back into focus, and when she shook her head to clear it, an explosion inside made her whimper and filled her stomach with bile. She gasped. She closed her eyes tightly. A finger touched her brow over her left eye, and she sucked in a breath at the fire there, at the dampness.

Doesn't matter; just a bump; doesn't matter.

Her feet were bare.

Her jeans were torn at both knees and in a slit across her buttocks.

The shirt she had bought only the day before had ripped along the left shoulder seam, gaped down the left side, and across the front were smears and smudges of dirt and blood, blades of dead grass when she'd fallen before, burrs, and over her right breast a clear handprint made of ash.

She felt the breeze, and it was cool.

She felt the tarmac's grit against her palms, against her knees, and she tried to rock back, to force herself to stand;

it wasn't that far to the top of the rise, a hundred yards, it couldn't be more. But she couldn't move. She was frozen. Nothing worked.

She wanted to run.

Nothing worked.

Her head lowered again and she licked her lips, wiped a forearm over her mouth to get rid of the dirt.

Her elbows quivered with the effort to keep her arms locked.

Stand up; but she couldn't.

A truck's going to come, you'll get run over, stand up.

She tried; she couldn't.

And she hadn't seen a car for hours, and that one had been just a flare of headlamps slashing over a hilltop and swerving sharply south and fading. She hadn't even heard the sound of its engine.

Get up.

I can't.

Crawl, then; and she did.

Ten yards of pebbles and edges digging into her palms and knees before her right elbow gave out, and she hobbled like a dog that had broken its leg, holding the useless arm across her stomach; ten yards more, fifteen beyond that, and she was on her stomach. Pushing with her toes, the sides of her feet; pulling with her fingers that looked like claws in the soft summer night. Paying no attention to the pebbles and edges that dug into her breasts and belly, scraped along her chin when her neck refused to work.

Pretend you're in a desert; it isn't cool, it's hot, and the sand is pretty soft.

Her lips felt chapped, her tongue felt swollen, and desert or country road, she would kill the next man who tried to stop her from taking a bath. She hated being dirty almost as much as she hated the blood, and when she rested for a moment—she didn't dare rest any longer— she remembered her mother telling her that young ladies didn't get dirty, they were soiled, just a little. Just like they didn't sweat, they only perspired.

remember that, child; young ladies are different.

Her mother was a pain in the ass.

A cough packed with phlegm froze her for a moment, and she gagged, swallowed, and grimaced.

A bird called softly out of the dark, and she realized for the first time how quiet it was out here, how still. The only noise was the stop-and-go scrape of her body against the road, the occasional angry grunt when a hand slipped, a foot slipped, and when the breeze gusted, she could hear the hiss of leaves.

It wasn't comforting at all.

Another twenty yards and she had to rest again. Her feet had been torn to hanging shreds—she didn't have to look, she just knew it—and she would have to wait a long time until she could push again without screaming. So she laid her cheek against the warm roadbed and stared across the surface at the trees that lined the far side of the ditch into which the shoulder fell. What were they in this part of the country? she wondered. Oak, she supposed, and some sycamore and maple. Pines? Lots of pines. And pale columns among the dark ones suggested caged and single birch.

She stared so long, things moved back there. Things without shapes that drifted and darted between the boles and fell gently from the branches and grew eyes that stared back and reflected no light.

She blinked quickly, hard, and shifted, staring between

her outstretched arms toward the dark line that cut the world into sky and land.

Suppose there's nothing over there?

What will you do if there's nothing over there?

She bit down hard on the inside of her cheek, and the spark made her yelp softly; punishment for near surrender.

Don't be an idiot; there's a farm, so there has to be a house. If not right there, then close. Think for a minute—didn't you see it today? Didn't you see the house just over that hill?

When you were running?

No.

She bit down again.

I don't remember.

Fair enough, the breeze told her; fair enough.

She braced her feet and hands.

Not long now, girl, not long.

Something darted over her head, a quick slap of wings that made her hunch her shoulders.

Something stirred in the trees, and a hasty rush through fallen leaves.

Not long; don't stop.

At the top of the rise she sobbed and grinned and rolled onto her back, staring at the stars, sneering at the moon.

It was there. It was dark. Midway down the steeper far slope. No trees, just open land, and a car in the driveway. The barbed-wire fence had been replaced by split rail.

Don't fall asleep.

I won't; God, I won't. Just give me a minute, I've got to get it together. Deep breaths, save your strength, you're almost there, you're almost home. On the count of three, don't screw it up now.

"One," a whisper to put her on her stomach.

"Two," a sigh as she wobbled to her hands and knees.

A grunted "three," as she stood and swayed, arms out and fingers stretching to snare her balance, determined not to fall because she'd be damned if she had come this far just to break her neck. Letting the hill take her down, turning sideways so she wouldn't fall, refusing to allow the pain in her soles, the pain in her side, the pain that had taken fierce root inside her skull to stop her. It wanted to. It wanted her to sleep, to slide through the fence and lie down over there in the cool silvered grass and let the cool grass bring her peace.

She wanted to, but she didn't want to die even more.

So she thought nothing, concentrating on the bobbing outline of the house over there, on the right. Searching the rails for the first opening, and in finding it staggered toward it, and in going through it felt the tarmac change to packed earth ridged and rutted.

It almost felt soft.

She skirted the car, not wanting to touch it, and paused for a moment at the bottom of the steps that led to a roofless, railed porch that was more like a low sundeck.

The place was a single-story clapboard, two windows on either side of a narrow wood-frame screen door, a chimney, an attached garage. There was no telling how deep it was. Shrubs along the foundation, and maybe flowers, she couldn't tell. It was as simple as a place could get without being a cabin.

It wasn't abandoned.

Someone was here.

She swallowed, swallowed twice, and took the three steps one at a time.

Cool; the wood was cool and smooth.

She leaned against the wall and fumbled with her right hand until she found the bell just to the right of the screen door.

Her head hurt, felt like fire.

She couldn't think.

I'm sorry, she thought, and she pushed it; honest to God, I'm really sorry.

No one answered; she wasn't surprised. It was at least two hours past midnight, maybe more. She didn't know. She pushed again, and this time held the plastic button in, listening to a muffled buzzing that proved the button worked.

She didn't drop her hand when a hooded bulb flared on over the lintel, forcing her to squint and turn her head; she didn't drop her hand when she heard someone fumbling with a lock on the inner door.

She waited until it opened and a shadow filled the screen before stepping away, arms limp, legs ready to collapse beneath her.

"What the hell do you want?" It was a man. "Christ, do you know what time it is?"

She stretched her right arm out, turned her bloody palm to the sky. "Help me," she whispered hoarsely. "Help me. Please."

Though she couldn't see a face, she could sense a puzzled frown.

"Lady? You okay?"

"Help me. Please. Help me."

Her right leg almost buckled, and she stumbled to one side, caught herself on the top rail before she fell.

"Lady?"

"Help me."

The screen door opened soundlessly, and he stepped

outside, caution in the way he watched her. He was taller than she, and thick across the chest and stomach. Naked from the waist up, jeans and bare feet, the jeans zipped but not buttoned, he wasn't wearing a belt. The overhead light shadowed his face, but his hair, mussed from sleeping, was thick and swept back, white or grey.

"Jesus, miss, what the hell happened?"

He took her arm gently and stared into her face, then shook his head at the damage he saw to her clothing.

"Help me," she whispered.

The hand slipped from her arm to her waist and he eased her inside, telling her to take it easy, one step at a time, not asking questions except with his eyes. His free hand slapped on a light and she saw a short hallway, doors left and right near the entrance, and again near the back where another door led, she assumed, into the back yard.

She stumbled.

"Easy," he said.

Nothing on the pine walls.

"Back here, can you make it?"

Nothing on the hardwood floors.

He brought her into a small bedroom, eased her onto the mattress of a double bed, and she sobbed at the cool soft sheets, at the pillow, at the overwhelming feeling that she hadn't made it after all, that somehow, between there and here, she had failed, and she had died.

Look, I'm not a doctor," he said, deep voice apologetic but determined to do something.

She shook her head carefully; it didn't matter. All she wanted was for the pain to go away, just long enough to let her sleep.

"If this hurts . . ."

She almost laughed.

Her eyes fluttered closed as he looked her over in the dim glow of a small bedside lamp. It was safer in there, in the dark spotted with flashes of pale color. But she could hear him apologizing for the phone not working, and for his clumsiness. He would do the best he could to make her comfortable.

"Anything broken? Your head, I think you may . . . Were you . . . uh . . . did someone . . ."

She shook her head again, lashes fluttering at the pain that nearly made her blind. What a beautiful voice. Not pretty, not quite hoarse.

He was gone, then, but before she panicked, she heard the sweet sounds of repair: running water in a sink, the soft warmth of a cloth that moved across her face, her hands and arms, her feet; hissing as he saw the road's debris clinging to her skin; muttering as he plucked the shards and pebbles out with tweezers, sparking single flames that died as soon as they were born. The cloth again, and it felt so damn good. Whistling tunelessly to himself, and apologizing every ten seconds for a real or imagined hurt.

She didn't move.

She let him have her.

She didn't stiffen when he unfastened her jeans and pulled them too slowly off her legs; she didn't fight when he unbuttoned her shirt and draped it open, when he gently, ever so gently, pushed her hair away from her brow.

Yes, she thought when he inhaled sharply at the sight; tell me about it.

Warm cloth, warm water.

The dirt was going away.

A gentle air pocket easing her down as he sat on the edge of the mattress, working on her stomach, breathing softly through his mouth.

"I think it looks worse than it is."

Don't you believe it, she thought, but she didn't open her eyes.

"You fell a long way, it looks like." He chuckled when she didn't answer. "Or somebody whipped you a good one with a birch rod."

She managed a smile. It wasn't much, she felt it waver, but it made him happy, and she didn't want him to stop. The sharpest pain had finally been banished, replaced by an aching lodged deep in her bones and muscles, and for the first time since moonrise she was able to let herself think of something else besides the screaming.

That's when she opened her eyes.

He was there, wringing a soiled cloth into a plastic bucket. He had thrown a shirt on, but hadn't buttoned it, and the thickness she had noticed earlier was clearly un-toned muscle, a middle-aged man who had nothing to prove by looking like a god. His face wasn't smooth; he spent a lot of time outdoors. His hair was white, not grey, and she bet herself it had been that way for more years than he wanted. When he turned his head, she tried a smile; when he smiled back, her own smile worked.

"Jim," he said. "Jim Scott."

"Rachel."

He nodded, and she saw him caught by her eyes, pale and dark—*your best feature, dear, don't tart them up, you know how you get*—until he blinked, frowned, reached to the footboard and unfolded a sheet over her. It was impossibly soft, and her hands clutched it, felt it, wondered if it was flannel. Not that she cared now. She could feel the exhaustion working its swift way from sole to aching shoulder, blurring her vision as he stood and watched her.

"It's close to dawn," he said at last. "Sleep as long as you want. You're going to need it. I'll go into town later, get some more disinfectant. You want to see a doctor?"

"No," she answered, but not too quickly. "I think . . . I think I'll be okay."

"That bump. Could be a concussion."

"No. I just want to . . . no."

His smile was one-sided—*your funeral*—and he closed the door behind him.

Leaving her alone, in the dark.

With the moon.

W̲ith the roar of an engine, a beast, and bobbing, swinging white lights that may have been eyes but they were so damn big and so damn bright, and an abrupt silence that wasn't quiet at all but filled with tiny noises

as the white eyes, the white lights, snapped off and there
was nothing left but the dark.

With the silence.

With the moon.

With the certainty even in sleep that someone was out
there, just waiting for her to die.

In the silence.

With the moon.

And with the sun when she awoke, pushing a glaring
halo around the shade pulled over the pane to the sill. It
was late morning, early afternoon, but it felt just like
twilight, and she eased the sheet away to examine herself,
paying no attention to the fragments of the dream lurking
still in the corners.

Dreams end.

She was still here.

She looked at herself and didn't know whether it was
finally time to cry.

God, she thought; good God.

Except for her panties, she was naked, and she could see it all.

She inhaled slowly, hissing quietly as she traced the bruises and scratches laced across her body. Then she prodded a little with her left hand, testing her rib cage, her hips, bracing herself awkwardly on one elbow as she poked at her thighs. Her right knee throbbed; her ankles were slightly swollen; and she felt as if she had lost a hundred pounds during the night.

a lady carries her weight properly, no matter how much she weighs.

She sighed. Her mother was, not to be unkind, fat; she herself had always been willow slender. Not much for the men to look at these days, and certainly not now.

But at least she wasn't dead.

Another ache brought a finger over her brow, trembling as it traced the swelling there, not daring to probe the lump itself. But the size of it made her whimper; an inch or two lower, and she wouldn't have that left eye.

Blinded like that, there was no question, she would die.

Slowly, very slowly, swallowing hard and fast, she sat all the way up, and carefully, very carefully, rubbed her eyes until she could see without sparks and rockets, then held her breath until her stomach surged and settled. The room was as small as she had supposed it was: just large enough for the single bed, a pine dresser, a trunk against the wall beside the dresser, a ladder-back chair and night-stand beside the bed. Nothing on the floor. Nothing on the walls.

A tickle in her throat made her cough once, and she was about to try to stand and find the bathroom, when she saw a tray on the nightstand, a glass, and a clear pitcher of water with condensation on the sides. When she touched it, it was cool; when she drank, it was heaven.

And as she drank, she listened for the voice of the house, and heard nothing.

She cocked her head.

He was gone.

Suddenly she yawned. Stretched carefully. Pointed her toes. Ignored the jabs of protest in joints and along her bones. Then she lay back down and pulled the sheet to her chin. Though the door was closed, she could feel a draft of cool air, scanned the walls again and discovered a small vent up near the ceiling. Central air, she thought; must be nice.

Well, he was nice too, so she supposed it all worked out. What she had to do now was rest, banish the aches and stinging, clear her head so she could think, and in thinking, figure out what to do next. Meanwhile, she allowed the weight of sleep to return to her side, sinking her back into the mattress, back into the down pillow, back to the country where the moon didn't reside.

Silence only.

No dreams.

No moon.

No great white beast with white staring eyes.

And out again, into a room that had furnished itself with shadows while she slept.

She sat up abruptly, alarmed, and was about to swing her legs over the edge of the mattress when dizziness spun her vision and slammed her back to the pillow. She gasped and pressed the heels of her hands to her temples, squeezing out the pain that replaced the spinning.

I'm going to throw up.

Deep slow breaths through her open mouth. Staring blindly at the ceiling. A palm that cupped her belly until at last the nausea passed.

Girl, she thought, you're not going anywhere.

When the door opened a few minutes later, she grabbed the sheet and yanked it to her chin, knowing it had been Jim who had undressed her, but this wasn't quite the same.

"How you doing?"

"Awful."

"Happens when you get beat up like that." He swung the chair away from the wall, turned it, and sat with his arms folded over the low back. "You sure you don't want a doctor?"

She nodded, and wished she hadn't. Her eyes closed. She swallowed convulsively, almost in a panic.

"There's a bowl on the floor there," he said. "Just in case you don't make it."

"Thanks," she managed.

"No problem." She heard him breathing, felt him watching her. "They fixed the line this morning. I can bring a phone in if you want. Someone you need to call?"

She thought of Momma, and shook her head.

"Then you want to tell me what happened?"

She wanted to sit up, but her head and stomach wouldn't let her; she wanted to stare out the window but the fading light was still too bright around the edges of the shade; she thought of telling him to mind his own business. Despite what he had done for her, she didn't feel an obligation. He had saved her, nothing more.

Her eyes opened, but she didn't say a thing.

He rested his chin on his arm. "See, the reason I ask, and I know it's not really any of my business, but I was over there this afternoon." He gestured vaguely over his shoulder. "Potar Ridge. It's a place where the kids go when they want to mess around without being hassled. You know the kind of place? So I was up there, checking around, and I ran into Maurice Lion." He grinned, and raised an eyebrow. "You don't know Maurice, but he's a hell of a guy. Black fella, always wears a white suit even in the middle of winter. I told him, Maurice, you get lost in a blizzard, we ain't gonna find you till spring. Tallest man I ever saw, too. And not a stitch of hair on his head. He shaves it every morning." He laughed quietly, shook his head. "He also happens to be a preacher."

She watched his features shift as the light dimmed and the room freed the rest of its shadows. The lines were still there, and the set of his jaw, but he didn't look the same anymore. She wasn't sure yet if she ought to be afraid.

"Anyway, old Maurice, he's been trying to set himself a big brass cross up there. To keep the sinners away, he says. I say he just wants to advertise his chapel, which is down the road a bit more, a couple of miles. You can see the Ridge from the interstate on a good day. But when I saw him, he was stomping around, hollering, shaking his fists at heaven, you never saw him so you don't know how scary that can be."

She didn't know, but she could imagine it. It was in his tone, and the way his eyes narrowed slightly.

"So naturally, I asked him what the hell he was doing, scaring all the crows and critters halfway to Kentucky, and he starts yelling about the place being desecrated, how the sinners have ruined the divine perfection of his natural temple—that's what he called it, his natural temple—and how he'd probably have to perform an exorcism to cleanse it before he could put up the cross.

"So I asked him again. Maurice, what in God's name are you foaming about?

"Jim, he said, they were using that rock and roll here last night. You know the kind I mean, the kind that calls up the Devil and makes children crazy.

"Maurice has a thing about rock 'n' roll.

"Anyway, he goes over to the edge and points, nearly falling over he was so angry. It's not a far drop, and it's not very steep, but I could see that a car had smashed through the brush, knocked over a couple of saplings. When I looked down, I saw it, and damn if the radio still wasn't playing. Hell of a battery. Took me most part of two hours just to calm him down and send him home."

He looked at her squarely.

"I climbed down there, Rachel, after he left. The car had been stripped pretty clean except for that dumb radio. No suitcases, no nothing. You know how far it is from there to here?"

She felt nothing; she shook her head.

"A couple three miles, give or take, going the long way around. Damn, but that's one hell of a walk out there. In the middle of the night."

A nervous hand fussed through the tangles of her hair.

"Tell you what," he said, swinging easily to his feet. "You think about it, I'll get you something to eat."

"Oh God, no," she said quickly, stomach already churning. "I don't think I could—"

"Soup, that's all," he answered. "You gotta have something."

He left before she could protest again, leaving the hall door ajar, letting in the light as the light outside drifted back over the mountains. Her hands fisted, she drew her lower lip between her teeth. She hated this, the helplessness, and worse because she was in the house of a . . . stranger wasn't quite the right word, but it was close enough, for now. Considering all that had happened, she was a little surprised she felt as safe as she did; considering all that had happened, all that still could, she was surprised she wasn't screaming.

He was back so quickly it took her a moment to realize she'd been dozing. She blinked rapidly to wake herself up, and smiled when she saw the tray in his hands, and the long T-shirt draped over his shoulder. He put the tray on the nightstand and dropped the T-shirt on the mattress.

"Make yourself decent," he said with a lopsided smile. "I'll be back in a second."

She did, smelling him on the cloth and shivering a little before sitting up and easing the tray across her legs. There was buttered bread, crackers, and a bowl of soup that smelled wonderful, and as she took the first taste—nearly laughing aloud; it was chicken noodle from a can—he returned with a sandwich in one hand, a bottle of beer in the other. He took his seat the same way, set the bottle on the floor, and watched her fumble with the first spoonful.

"You want me to help?"

She looked at him without raising her head. "I haven't been fed since I was a baby."

He shrugged.

She ate, not realizing how hungry she had been until her stomach ceased its rebellion and let itself be filled.

They didn't speak.

In the middle of a swallow, she thought: If I tell him, I'll scream.

It nearly choked her.

Aware of his watching, she took her time, trying to decide what she ought to do. She had no idea why he hadn't called the police, especially after he had discovered the car and its condition; and there was no way she was going to trust this man blindly. But she still didn't know. He hadn't touched her, not that way, and he hadn't demanded answers. A quick smile, there and gone. Well, it wasn't exactly a demand, but he did want to know, and if she didn't tell him something that was at least vaguely plausible, he'd probably . . . what?

She didn't know that either.

So maybe she ought to just tell him the truth.

young ladies don't lie, dear, they embroider; and they never tell the whole truth if they can avoid it, and that's why you'll make one very fine leader one of these days.

Oh, Momma, she thought wearily, why the hell don't you stay away?

So what to do, damnit?

Play it by ear; there was really no other choice.

Besides, you got away from them once, you can do it again if you have to.

He finished the sandwich, leaned over to pick up the bottle, and froze when she said calmly, "They tried to kill me."

T he silence was so great, she almost tipped the tray over when he set the bottle back down and looked at her, not quite frowning.

"Who?" he asked.

She stared so fiercely at the soup bowl that her eyes began to water, and she slapped them dry with a finger, not wanting him to think the memory made her cry. It could have; she just didn't want it to.

What it did was make her mad.

"It's okay, you know," he told her calmly. "If it's private business, something like that, you don't have to say anything. You don't owe me."

Jesus, she wondered, what the hell is this guy?

But she knew that one already.

She rubbed a finger briskly beneath her nose, then over her upper lip, before gesturing that she wanted her legs free to move. He moved quickly, taking up the tray, putting it on the nightstand, pulling another pillow from the dresser's bottom drawer so she could sit up without slumping.

He sat.

He watched.

She couldn't help thinking of a big old dog, lying on a porch, just waiting for her to notice him.

But she knew in that same moment this big old dog had very large teeth.

It unnerved her and, without understanding why, made her feel safe.

It shouldn't have; it definitely shouldn't have.

She focused on the open doorway.

"I've been living in Los Angeles the past year or so," she began when she didn't think her voice would crack, "and decided to come home for a while. Virginia, that's where I used to live. Just outside Richmond."

Nothing had worked out. Aspirations of stardom, then minor stardom, then any part she could find didn't die hard, they just took a long time dying. Playing the game didn't work because she couldn't keep track of the rules, and she had a disturbing penchant for saying what was on her mind instead of what she was supposed to tell those who pretended to listen. So she fell back on her degree to do some paralegal work until she'd made up her mind what the hell she really wanted; and when she decided she would rather starve in a familiar place than under the sun in California, she sold what she could, gave away the rest, and bought a used car to take her home.

Y ou know what it's like, she asked, plucking idly at the sheet, driving all night? I don't know, it's weird sometimes. Nothing looks like it's supposed to. Every time you think you're where you want to be so you can stop and find a room, there's more highway up there. I probably should have flown, I had the money, but I had this stupid idea that I wanted to see the country. Thirty years old and not getting any younger, as my Momma used to say, so I decided to take the chance. Traveling alone, for a woman, is about as dumb a thing as you can do, I guess, but Momma always said Corder women were pioneers, so I figured what the hell.

I saw them first just outside Nashville, on the way from Memphis.

I went to Graceland, you know. God. There were kids there, crying at his grave. Kids! He's been dead longer than some of them have been alive. You ever been to Lourdes? I have a feeling it's something like that. I kept looking for the place where they keep the crutches people don't need anymore. It was spooky. I couldn't get out of there fast enough.

Three hours later, I decided to stop in Nashville and see some things, nothing special, and this really huge old Cadillac comes drifting up behind me. I mean, it was like an ocean liner with giant fins, and it must be thirty years old if it's a day. I was doing sixty-five in the right lane, and that bastard driver, you should have seen him, he tailgated me for I don't know how long. I tried slowing down to get him to pass, but he wouldn't. I stopped for gas, and he was right there when I got back on the interstate.

It's the first time since I left California that I really got nervous. The truck drivers didn't bother me, the kids, nothing did, not really. I've had guys play stupid highway tag with me before, but this guy . . . Jesus.

Then, just outside the city, he went away.

I only stayed for a couple of days. I couldn't stand it

anymore. You ever been there? Everything is Loretta
Lynn this and Merle Haggard that, and some woman I
never heard of has got a chain of discount drug stores, for
crying out loud, her picture out front and everything. It's
crazy. So after I got tired of it, I shopped for some new
clothes and had something for dinner, I figured I could
get to Roanoke, or close to it, before I got too tired to
drive anymore.

He picked me up again, about half an hour outside
Knoxville.

Look, I'd been driving the interstates for days, I was
touristed out, my eyes were crossed from looking at so
much blacktop, and I was just not in the mood for some
macho asshole trying to impress me with a refurbished
Caddy. I mean, it was gorgeous and all, I suppose, if you
like that sort of thing, but Jesus Christ, I was beginning to
wish I had a gun.

I could have shot him.

I could have shot them all.

I don't know what the hell I was thinking. Really. But
for some stupid reason I thought that if they thought I was
getting close to home, they'd stop bothering me and go
pick on someone else. I could see there were about four
of them in there, maybe five. Damn, did you know those
cars had so much room back then? It was hard to tell
exactly how many because of the sun. It was about down
by then, poking between the mountains behind us, and it
shone through his back window to the windshield and
made it look like silver one time, almost black the next.
So after I passed the Ashville junction, where the interstates come together—you know where it is? Where after
a while the highway starts all this up-and-down stuff

before it goes into Virginia?—after that, when I couldn't take him any longer, I decided to get off the first chance I got.

I turned left off the ramp and crossed over the highway.

He kept following.

Now I was scared. I knew I'd been a jerk, but I didn't dare stop because I realized they weren't playing anymore, and all I wanted to do was find a town, police station, anything where I could get out and get some help.

There wasn't any.

They started bumping me then.

We weren't going very fast, all those little roads kept twisting and turning, and he'd come up and nudge me a little. Not hard, but it made the wheel jump and a hell of a lot of noise and scared the shit out of me. I was screaming at him, and I was just screaming, you know? Then I found this place, this little side road and I took it.

I don't know why.

The car had started to smoke, and it was making all these banging and rattling noises, and I started to cry, and it had finally gotten dark, and all I could think of was that the son of a bitch was going to run me into a tree, and they were going to rape me. They wouldn't kill me. That wouldn't be any fun. They were just going to drag me out and rape me.

We climbed this mountain, hill, I don't know what the hell it was, and ran along this narrow road, hardly any room on either side, and suddenly it was pretty open, and the road didn't go anyplace except back the way I'd come.

The moon was out.

I could see for miles.

I could see the edge past the trees that were there.

I tried to stop and turn, all at the same time, and I ended up sideways to the edge.

That . . . that *thing* just sat there, dust floating all around it, and I was so hoarse I couldn't yell anymore, but I tried. God, I tried.

His headlights blinded me.

The engine . . . it was quiet, so quiet it sounded like . . . I don't know, but it didn't sound like a car.

And those headlights looked like eyes.

Then he came closer, and all I could think of was to lock the doors, then get ready to floor it when he came close enough.

I didn't have a chance.

He came closer, so close there was nothing but light in the window and I couldn't see a damn thing.

Everything had turned white.

I got ready to jam it, then, just waiting for him to open the door, but all I could hear was that engine, so quiet I couldn't believe it. It's dumb now, but it almost sounded like that car was breathing.

He just sat there.

And just when I decided I wasn't going to wait, there was just enough room for me to go forward and, if I turned tight and fast enough, get around him before he could block me . . . he moved.

The son of a bitch nudged me again.

Then he pushed me over the side.

And you know what?
He was laughing.
All the time we sat there, I could hear him laughing.

Oh Jesus, Jim, look at me, I'm shaking.

I don't know how close to the bottom that damn car went, but all I could think of was thank God I was wearing my seatbelt. Jesus. I was going to die, get blown up or crushed or something, and all I could think of was that damn seatbelt.

Then I stopped rolling and sliding, and I was out of there. I didn't have time to find out if I was hurt. I just got out of there and ran.

There were so many trees I couldn't see, and there were bushes that had all kinds of thorns, and I don't know how many times I fell, must've been a thousand, and that goddamned moon was bright enough for sunlight.

And I could hear them laughing.

All the time I ran, I could hear them laughing.

And then . . . hell, I don't know, I guess I lost them.

I knew I was getting away and that made me run harder and I was so fucking scared, you don't know how scared I was, and they were still laughing back there.

Christ.

All the time, the whole goddamn time I could hear them laughing.

Like . . . I don't know, like . . .

Jackals," he said quietly. "They sound just like jackals."

Under the moon they rode the interstate, climbing toward Bristol and Virginia as the Blue Ridge Mountains closed close around them.

A long white Cadillac with glaring white eyes.

The two men in back, both young and both in jeans and plaid shirts, dozed fitfully. The blond, with a thin blond mustache nearly invisible in daylight, muttered something, licked his lips, and tucked himself into the corner; the other one, much larger and darker, had a knee propped up against the seat in front. His long hair covered half his face, and the wide scar etched from the corner of his right eye to the corner of his mouth.

The driver shook his head wearily. "How we going to work if they won't stay awake."

The passenger patted his knee. "Don't fret so much, Willum, you'll get gray before your time."

Willum grinned. "Long as what I got hangs around long enough to get gray, I guess I won't mind."

A pickup sped past them. Even in the dark they could see the exhaust cloud behind it.

"Damn," Willum said quietly. "That's the first thing we've seen in nearly an hour." He shifted, and rubbed a hand over his face. "I think it's a waste, Ruby."

Ruby agreed with a soft grunt.

"So?" he asked.

She backed against the door. "So maybe we go back, find out where the fawn went."

"We know."

"Maybe. Maybe not."

"We know," he insisted without raising his voice.

"So maybe we ought to make sure."

They rode on.

Willum's hands tightened on the beveled wheel. "And what if she found him?"

"Well," she said, drawing out the word as she watched the road speed toward them, "maybe we just ought not to count our chickens before they're dinner. Things happen, you know. Could be, things happen."

"We going back?" a graveled, tired voice asked from the back seat.

Ruby nodded as Willum took the Caddy to an off-ramp.

"We going to see him?"

She nodded again.

Before response could be made, Willum said, "We'll find a place to rest, get something to eat." He smacked his lips loudly. "Fried chicken, dumplings, gravy, ow!" when Ruby smacked him hard on the arm.

"Watch your mouth," she scolded.

He looked at her.

She laughed.

The Caddy swept back onto the highway, heading west, all alone.

Nothing in its wake but the sound of something laughing.

He had seen it in those amazing pale-dark eyes the night before—the terror of irrational pursuit, and the mild shock that went with it, although she probably didn't realize it. Deer-scared in the headlights, except she hadn't run, and she certainly wasn't soft, and those eyes didn't belong to any deer he knew. Now he saw it all again when he spoke—the spastic twitch of a small muscle in her cheek that pulled the corner of her mouth back just a little, and the jerk of her right hand as she stared at him and debated whether or not she was fast enough to get away.

She had escaped once; she could do it again.

What to say. What to do to help her.

How do you explain a nightmare so the nightmare isn't a dream?

She blinked so rapidly, he thought for a second she was going to faint.

Then she cleared her throat. "You know them?" Hoarsely: "You know who they are?"

He drank, and wiped his upper lip with a finger. "I'm not sure. Maybe."

She struggled to sit up again, and he held out a palm, not touching her but putting her gently back to her pillow. "There's some older boys, I think they're from around Knoxville, they ride the roads and get their kicks from scaring the hell out of tourists."

Her face darkened. "This was more than just scaring."

He nodded carefully. "I can see that." He scratched his

cheek, the bottle still in his hand. "Drinking, sounds to me, don't you think? I have to admit, though, I don't know everything they do. It's their reputation, you know what I mean?" Another drink, the bottle was empty.

"No," she said.

"I mean, there's stuff they could be getting away with, nobody knows about it, they can only guess." He set the bottle down beside the chair.

Her eyelids fluttered as she fought to stay alert. "So you didn't call the cops?"

He looked at her for several seconds, trying to judge just how much of a city girl she really was. "Sometimes, around here, it's more . . . effective . . . when some things get handled on their own."

He wasn't sure, but he thought she was both shocked, and that she approved. They had touched her, those men had, in places she probably didn't know about, and most certainly didn't approve.

He had been touched too long ago to care.

Not long enough to forget.

The sun was gone; only the small lamp, and a fainter glow from the hall.

"A name."

"What?"

She looked at him, the dim light streaking her face with shadowed lines. She seemed a lot older; he suspected sadly she was.

"A name. Do these 'boys' have a name?"

"Modeen," he answered without hesitation. Then he added, "Pricks, the whole family."

"Yeah. Tell me about it."

No, he thought; not if you want to get home alive.

She groaned suddenly, hissed with drawn-back lips,

and closed her eyes as she twisted away from one hip. He
was on his feet quickly, pushing the chair out of the way,
but she shook her head, lifted a staying hand.

"Ache, you said?"

He waggled a hand side to side.

She snorted. "Try misery."

He told her to hang on a minute, he'd be right back.
He took the tray and bottle and brought them into the
kitchen, grabbed a shot glass from a cupboard over the
stove, and hurried into the bathroom. There he filled
the glass from a bottle in the medicine cabinet.

Not thinking.

Not daring.

In the bedroom she had pressed back into the pillows,
staring at the ceiling.

"You all right?"

Her smile was brief and mocking.

"Sorry." He handed her the glass.

She frowned at the pale red liquid. "What's this?"

"Phenobarb." He took the chair again. "It tastes awful,
so chug it. It'll calm you enough to sleep."

"I thought you weren't a doctor."

He shook his head, grinning. "Not quite. But you've
obviously got yourself a little concussion there, like I said.
Plus you're beat up, and you still hurt like holy hell. You
slept before because you were exhausted from all that
running. Now you're healing. A good sleep isn't going to
be that easy for a while."

She drank, grimaced, and handed him the empty glass.
"Not a doctor, huh? Lots of experience, though."

He shrugged with one shoulder.

She adjusted the pillows and sighed loudly.

"Who are you?" she asked softly.

"Jim Scott."

"I know that." Her lips moved, trembling for words. "But who are you?"

He stood, moved the chair back to its place against the wall, and settled the light blanket over her. "A friend," he answered, just as softly.

"Hope so."

So do I, he thought as he switched off the light.

"Leave the door open?"

"Sure."

He stood in the hallway and looked at her, all in shadow now, just a form on the bed.

And just before he turned away, his expression turned to stone.

Once in the living room, he dropped into an old leather armchair deliberately angled so he could glance out the large front window while he read, or listen to a ballgame while sitting in the dark.

It was a simple room, with an ordinary two-cushion couch facing the curtain-framed picture window. No pictures or travel posters, nothing on the floor, the furniture doing nothing more than doing its job—a low filled bookcase, a packed magazine rack, a low metal stand with a small-screen TV, a sideboard dressed with glasses and several bottles of liquor, another chair that matched and faced his, and end tables that held lamps that didn't match at all.

He was tired.

He had spent most of last night sitting right here, staring out at the road.

Waiting.

Dozing until the sun rose.

After checking on Rachel, he had eaten, and after the phone line had been repaired, he had made a few calls. Once done with business, he had had every intention of driving into town to find out what, if anything, anyone had heard about the Modeens. Instead, he had dozed off on the couch and hadn't awakened until he'd heard her stirring.

That unnerved him.

Sleeping like that, at a time like this, was going to get him killed.

Now, he pressed the heels of his hands against his temples and pressed, *pushed,* creating sparks that banished any temptation to close his eyes again.

Bad business, he thought as his hands lowered to his lap; just when you think you've got it all set, everything ready, something comes along and makes it look all wrong.

He coughed quietly.

You're feeling sorry for yourself.

He shook his head.

Nope; just feeling stupid.

He took the telephone from the side table and set it on his lap, and was about to call Maurice, to get some comfort and pass the word, when it rang, nearly stopping his heart, forcing him to hold his breath.

"Jesus," he whispered, throat abruptly dry, staring at the instrument as if he'd never seen one before. "Get hold, you idiot, get hold."

The telephone rang.

He didn't want to pick it up.

Not this time of night.

J im?"

He tucked the receiver between ear and shoulder and twisted around so he could look out the window. The moon. He kept his voice low.

"Charlie, for God's sake, that you?"

He propped his feet up on the sill, grinning.

"In the flesh, in the flesh."

He grinned, reached for a cigarette, and remembered he'd left the pack in his bedroom.

"Well, where the hell are you?"

The field across the road was silver and black.

"Birmingham."

Something moved out there.

"Son of a bitch, no kidding? You coming up this way, I hope. It's been a hell of a long time, man. Maurice's going to have a fit. And Nola and Jonelle, all they ever do is talk about—"

Charlie Acres coughed as though he were bringing up his lungs. Jim winced at the familiar painful sound and waited, left hand on the armrest, fingers drumming.

Out in the field, moving right to left, something dark passed through the high grass. It was too distant to tell size, but it was larger than a big dog.

"They're here, Jim," Acres said hoarsely when the spasm passed. "They're here."

Jim didn't blink. "Who?"

"Santa Claus and his elves. Who the fuck do you think, man? The Modeens. They're here."

Jim blew softly. His chest, stomach, groin tightened, and the muscles of his right arm twitched once. "I'll be damned. Which ones?"

There was a pause, the sound of the receiver changing hands, and he could hear the distant muffled sound of passing traffic, the blare of an eighteen-wheeler. Acres was at a pay phone, probably on a highway.

"Best I can figure . . . all of them."

Oh Jesus.

He snapped his head around, staring at the hall in case Rachel had heard him. He strained, eyes narrowed, but he didn't think she was there. With any luck at all, she'd sleep through the night. Like the dead.

"Jim?"

"Here, bud. Look, you sure it's all? I think I got some of them up here too."

"Shit."

His fingers stopped; his feet dropped soundlessly to the floor.

Something big, streaking through the field.

Something large.

"Charlie, you've got to get your ass to my place pronto. If you're right—"

Acres coughed again, worse than before, worse than Jim had ever heard. A touch of cold traced across his chest.

"Jim?" Gasping now; hardly able to breathe.

"Still here, pal. Now do me a favor and hang up, get to your car, and—"

"I can't."

"Don't be stupid, Charlie."

"I can't. They've seen me, Jim. Spotted me this afternoon, I think, when I stopped for gas. I don't know if I
can make it that far."

"Then fly, for Christ's sake. You don't need to take the
roads. You need money, I'll wire it."

"I don't know."

Jim's throat dried; it felt like straw down there.

"Jim? Shit. Look, there's more. I heard—"

"Charlie, forget it. Tell me when you—"

"It's not just them, Jim. The Modeens. I was in this
diner last night, the most godawful meat loaf you ever had
in your life, and I—"

He heard a faint, high-pitched whistling, a winter's
wind in fallen leaves, and Acres whispered something he
couldn't catch just before the line went dead.

"Charlie?"

The shadow in the field passed out of sight.

"Charlie?"

Something flew across the moon.

Something large.

As silently as he could, he set the receiver on its cradle,
eased the phone to the floor, and pushed himself to the
edge of the cushion, leaning forward, elbows on his
thighs, hands in a single fist beneath his chin. His forehead
nearly touched the pane as he stared at the road, at the
field, watching the moon bleach the stars.

I'm not ready, he thought; please, God, I'm not ready.
they tried to kill me.

I'm not.

they laughed like . . .

He had fallen asleep last night when he should have been awake.

"Charlie," he whispered.

He hoped it wasn't a eulogy, found a star, made a wish and astonished himself by believing.

Just drive, you son of a bitch, he told the dark; just get in that damn car and drive, you hear?

He dragged the phone over between his feet, watched the moon for a while, then dialed.

J onelle? It's Jim."

"Well, damn, do you have any idea what time it is?"

Jonelle Ryman, a little woman with a deep voice and black eyes and hair to match. Standing with him, she barely came up to the middle of his chest; standing with Maurice, she looked like a toddler until she turned around. Not even a blind man would mistake her for a child. She had a tendency to wear clothes that emphasized that face, and rode a motorcycle that, rolled over, would crush her like a gnat.

"Peter around?"

"That's it? You call in the middle of the night, practically dawn, for God's sake, and I don't even get a 'hey, Jonelle, what's new?' "

He smiled. "Last time I saw you was three days ago. What could be new?"

"I could've run off with the garbageman, been hit by a truck, drowned, you name it."

He glanced outside. "Hey, Jonelle, what's new?"

She hesitated. "You sound awful."

"Peter," he answered.

She swore and covered the mouthpiece, but he could hear her calling her younger brother. Owner of the gas station on the interstate intersection.

When he came on, he was coughing sleep from his throat. "It better be good."

"Modeen."

The silence matched the night.

Then Peter said, "Aw, shit."

"Yeah. Just heard from Charlie Acres."

Peter made a noise; Jim could imagine him shaking his head.

"Where?"

"Birmingham, for sure."

"Here?"

Moonlight made him squint. "I'm not sure. Maybe. There's more, I'll tell you later."

"Wonderful. Goddamn . . . wonderful."

"The tow truck?"

"Damn, Jim, you really need it now?"

"No. Soon, though. I reckon about . . . I don't know. Soon."

"Consider it done."

"Thanks. And tell Jonelle."

"Hell, she's probably listening in down in the kitchen."

"I am not!"

Jim almost laughed aloud. Something about that

woman; there was just . . . something about that woman.

"Sleep well, you two."

"Oh, sure," Peter grumbled. "Right."

The young man hung up, Jonelle a moment later.

Jim pushed the phone away with his foot, and stared at the moon.

He didn't bother to look at his watch when he finally roused himself and stood, rubbing at the small of his back to relieve the stiffness that had grown there. But he guessed that daybreak wasn't all that far away.

A yawn took him by surprise, but he didn't feel tired; nevertheless, there was no question he had to rest. To-morrow—today, he corrected—he had to do something about Rachel Corder. If she felt better, if he thought she could travel, he figured the best thing would be to bring her over to Tri-City Airport, get her on the first plane to Richmond, if that's where she was headed. It wouldn't be easy. She didn't have any money, that had been taken with the rest of her things, and he doubted she was the kind to take anything from strangers.

He grunted a laugh as he stood outside his bedroom, looking at her doorway. He couldn't see anything from here, but he could feel her, and he moved quietly across the hall to the threshold, looked in and saw that she'd rolled over to her side, one arm dangling over the mat-tress.

When she moaned in her sleep, he backed away guilt-ily, up on his toes. Sleep is private; no one should watch you sleep, no matter how romantic the romantics make it seem.

Sleeping, Maurice had once said, is temporary dying; and no one should watch you die, either.

Especially not a stranger.

He tapped his forehead sharply to drive off the morbid thought, yawned again, and scratched his belly as he went into his own room, not bothering to switch on the light.

Stranger.

He shook his head.

After all this, it wasn't likely.

But that was something he'd work on later. Right now, he needed rest. Too much fat-of-the-land crap had gone under the bridge and to his waist since the first time, despite his efforts to stay in shape, and while he never considered himself old, seldom considered his age at all, there was the undeniable fact he was still getting older, getting slower. Adjustments would have to be made.

If they'd only give him time.

He undressed and raised the shade on his window, to use the sun as an alarm clock. Then he slipped shivering between the sheets, grunted, and closed his eyes with a silent sigh.

Time was something they never gave anyone, least of all him.

No, he corrected.

Especially him.

R uby shifted her massive weight uneasily when Willum returned to the car. He was a little out of breath, and she scolded him for taking such a stupid chance.

But all he said was, "I have an idea."

Ruby checked the back seat; the boys were sleeping hard, both of them snoring. "Tell me."

He did.

She shook her head, wondering why she had bothered to listen in the first place. He was good, Willum was, but he had never been able to see beyond the next nightfall.

"We have to know," he insisted.

"She's there."

"But we have to *know*."

She folded her arms under her breasts and stared thoughtfully through the windshield. The car was parked beneath a huge tree, whose low branches nearly hid them. She shook her head slowly. There was something not right about this, and she couldn't figure it out, and felt the anger grow again.

"We don't have much time," he reminded her softly.

"I know, I know! You think I don't know that?"

He glanced into the back. "It'll give the boys something to do."

She had to smile. "True, they'd love it."

"And you can trust them not to be stupid."

A chuckle. "Don't know about that." She opened the

door; the overhead light didn't work. "I got to run. I got to think."

"Not too long now."

She promised.

Not that she gave a damn.

Charlie, damnit, be here, Jim thought the second he opened his eyes and felt the sun. A moment later he frowned; the room was too dim. He turned his head and realized the shade had been lowered, the curtains drawn across it. When he grabbed his watch from the night table and squinted at it, he sat up quickly in disbelief and groaned; it was almost noon, and he'd been worried about Rachel needing sleep?

Jesus.

"Oh, good work, Scott," he told the room as he dressed. "Women and children first, but don't bother me, boys, until the ship starts to slide. I need my beauty rest."

When he hurried into the kitchen she was already there, toast in the making, coffee on the round pine table, bare feet, shirt untucked, her hair still damp from a recent shower.

And I didn't hear a thing, he thought; Jesus H, I didn't hear a thing.

He dropped into a chair and picked up his cup.

"You snore," she said from the counter.

"Nope."

"Trust me. You snore."

His gaze followed her from over the rim of the cup as she moved from place to place—"I ate hours ago, I'll just have some coffee"—knowing where most things were, guessing pretty good at the rest. When she sensed him watching, she held up a butter knife. "You say I'll make someone a good wife someday, I'll use this."

He grinned. "Never crossed my mind."

She grinned back. "Like hell."

She joined him as he ate, her cup gathered between her palms, and he wondered aloud if anyone had come to the door while he'd slept.

"No. You expecting a package?"

He shook his head, didn't explain.

how many?

She glanced around the room, then stretched, arms up and behind her head. "I feel . . ."

He waited.

She slumped, sighing. "Awful. But not as bad."

She looked much better. The scratches he could see weren't nearly as nasty as they had been, and she had hidden the temple bruise with the fall of her hair. Only the swelling above her eye gave her away; it was much smaller now, but the bruising had spread, black and yellow. There wasn't much she could do about that.

"I've been thinking about those people, the Modeens?"

Carefully, very carefully: "Okay."

"I guess you know what you're doing, not going to the police." She picked up a fork and pressed the tines lightly against her wrist. "I was mad at first, but then I figured things don't necessarily work down here the same as they do up in Richmond."

all of them

He was relieved, and did his best not to show it.

The tines pressed deeper; her fingers curled.

"But I'd like you to do something for me, okay?"

"If I can."

A nod, barely seen. "Okay. You've got to promise me *you'll* do something about it. Personally."

It was hard not laughing. "Rachel, that's the easiest promise I'll ever have to make."

She didn't smile.

Those eyes changed.

"I don't think you understand," she said flatly. "I want them hurt. I want them hurt bad."

"And I suppose you'll want proof?" He did laugh then, quickly, pushing a hand back through his hair. "An ear, a finger, something like that?"

She didn't laugh at all. "Something like that."

Brother, he thought; oh, brother.

Her chest and arms rose as she inhaled slowly and deeply, exhaled in a rush. The eyes changed again, and he could feel the room change as well.

"So," she said. "How the hell do I get home?"

That woman is too damn many people, he decided as he drank the last of his coffee. She was making him dizzy, and her cold-blooded demand hadn't been a joke, which made him both uneasy and a little curious. In a way he was sorry she was leaving; he wasn't sure he really wanted to know her much better than he already did, but at the same time, he had a feeling time with her wouldn't be boring.

Much as he didn't want to, he said, "I'm not so sure you're ready to travel just yet."

She stared at him for a long time, long enough to make him clear his throat, try to put it another way. But she beat him to it.

"Actually, I already thought of that. I'm still a little dizzy now and then, and I don't think my muscles are ever going to stop aching." The fork returned to its spot on the placemat. "But I don't want to put you to more trouble. God knows, you've done enough."

He had passed the test, whatever it was, and as he drained his cup, he feared he had made a mistake. But this was the second day after the chase, and they still hadn't shown up, so maybe, this time, it would be all right.

How do you know? You slept all night, half the day. How do you know?

"You all right?" she asked.

He nodded. "Just mad at myself, that's all. I didn't mean to sleep so long, leave you alone."

She leaned over the table to take his empty cup, but he stopped her with a wave. "You've done your bit. At least let me clean up."

She leaned back, folding her arms loosely across her chest. "I'm not going to argue."

"When I'm done," he said, gesturing toward the back, "I'll show you around. Give you a chance to keep those muscles from stiffening up too badly."

He was at the sink, rinsing the dishes, when she said, "So who are you, Jim?"

He looked over his shoulder.

"You're not from around here," she guessed, her voice startling him. Her accent, pure Virginia Richmond, had strengthened a little. "It's some words that don't really make it, if you know what I mean."

He dried the plate with a towel looped around the undersink cabinet handle. "Chicago."

"What?"

"Yep." His shrug was near apologetic. "Most of my young life there, right up through college and all. Too much, if you ask me again. Down here, though . . . I don't know. It doesn't take long to fall into the rhythm for someone like me. I heard one guy on TV a while back, I don't know where the hell he was from, he called it lazy talk. I call it easy talkin', no reason to work at it, you'll get where you're going sooner or later. For some Northerners and West Coasters I guess I do pass for a native." He winked at her. "It's the pure bloods that know I'm a fake."

"So what do you do?"

He turned and leaned back against the sink. "Kind of nosy, ain't you?"

"It's part of my charm." She met his gaze squarely. "So, you going to tell me?"

His hand rubbed his chin mock thoughtfully, and there was an explosion of humor in his eyes. "Well, sometimes I buy and sell land here and there, sometimes I don't do anything but scratch myself and get drunk, but mostly what I am, I guess, is goddamn rich."

She tried not to gape.

When the humor reached his lips, he laughed aloud, crossed the cool tiled floor, and took her arm to lead her back into the hall.

Finally she said, "You're kidding, right?"

He rapped a knuckle against the wall by her room, and stared pointedly at her feet. "Unless you want to put more holes in those things, maybe you ought to try the sneakers I left in the bedroom."

As she passed into the bedroom, he said, quite seriously, "No, Rachel. I'm not kidding."

A small porch like the porch in front faced a full-acre lawn. There was no fence out here, just meadow and pasture and climbing low hills that had reminded him of gumdrops the first time he'd seen them; a few old trees, two of which braced a canvas hammock between them, untouched woodland that bordered the lawn north and south. Far to their left was a ridge of mountains running east to west, summits smooth and jagged, slopes dark with trees and shadow.

They walked for an hour, stopping now and then, resting on a boulder or under a tree, while he tried to show her how much land he owned without spelling out the numbers, without sounding as if he was bragging. Mostly, he said, not exaggerating all that much, it was what they could see until a hill or mountain got in the way. She was impressed, and he felt foolish because, oddly, he was pleased at her reaction.

And when it was obvious she had neared the end of her strength, they returned to the house where he suggested, strongly, she take a nap.

"Tonight, when you get up, I'll take you to the finest meal this side of the Tennessee, maybe even the Mississippi. Then a good night's sleep, you'll be ready and home by dinnertime tomorrow."

She clearly wanted to argue, pride evidently not wanting to let him know just how bad she felt and how badly she needed the rest; but she agreed, yawned and laughed, and disappeared into the bedroom. As soon as he was sure she had settled down, he went to the living room, opened the liquor cabinet, and moved two bottles of brandy to one side. Then he slid a panel aside and took out a cloth bundle. He unwrapped it and hefted the exposed .38 in his hand. Loaded it. Tucked it into his belt, pulled his shirt out all around, put on a pair of sunglasses, and went outside.

The car was hot and stifling, the interior almost too hot to touch, and he cursed forgetting to roll down the windows. He considered driving back to the interstate, to a place he knew where he could watch the traffic without the traffic watching him, or to see if Jonelle and Peter had noticed anything, but he was afraid the engine's noise, never gentle at the best of times, would wake Rachel up.

So he walked instead, two miles south, the way she'd first come to him.

He didn't really expect to find anything, and he didn't, and became angry at the disappointment that flirted at the edges of his relief.

Back at the house, he showered, dressed, and waited in the living room.

Watching the sun go down.

Watching the field across the road.

Starting when she came into the room, smiling, declaring she was starved and if he didn't keep his promise, she'd eat everything in the cupboards.

"Not," she added wryly, "that I care all that much for chicken soup."

A quick hand over his face told him he needed a shave, and while he did, she leaned against the bathroom jamb, listening as he reckoned aloud she might even be able to get home in the morning. He gave her her choice of airports. Although he didn't believe she would have trouble getting the flight she wanted from Tri-City, he felt she'd be pleased to know there would be plenty of back-up over in Knoxville, just in case. The offer to supply her with the ticket was accepted without question or condition; a further offer of a little cash for minor expenses was also accepted without her protesting at all.

"Just don't expect me to be able to pay you back soon," she said on their way to the front door.

He smiled. "Your company, dear lady, is all the payment I expect."

She looked up at him and grinned. "Bullshit."

"Absolutely."

"You're really rich?"

"Disgusting."

"Maybe I won't pay you back at all."

But she would. This woman, like only a few others he had met who knew him and what he was, wouldn't accept an obligation unless she could meet it fairly.

With a wink, then, she pushed him aside and opened the door.

"Son of a bitch," she said, "it's *hot* out here!"

The telephone rang.

It could have been any number of people, calling this time of day—Maurice, Jonelle, a dozen others, but he had a bad feeling it wasn't. Charlie Acres hadn't arrived, and even if he'd been crawling, it wasn't that far from there to here. He should have been here by dawn, shortly after, if he was coming at all.

The telephone rang.

He closed his eyes briefly, a futile attempt to ignore it and dispel the feeling; he had even gone so far as to start to shut the door, but Rachel's quizzical look asked him if he was going to answer.

With a sigh he tossed her the car keys. "Start her up, okay? Get the air conditioner working. It's going to be a bitch in there."

She caught them, squeezed them, yet he felt her watching as he hurried back in, leaving the door open, and grabbed the receiver, standing in the window.

It didn't take very long—a state trooper out of Chattanooga had found Charlie's body on the shoulder of I-75, three miles beyond Lookout Mountain just after sunrise. The man calling was polite, very official, but Jim could hear the tremor and knew it was bad. Acres had Jim's name in his wallet as next of kin, hence the call and the questions, none of them accusatory, none out of line.

"Thank you," he said flatly when the man was done. "I'll take care of it."

He didn't remember hanging up, didn't hear Rachel return to the house.

It was bright out there, sunglasses bright, bright enough to bring a few salty tears to a man's eyes.

And the heat made it hard to breathe.

And the birds heading home to roost for the night made it hard to think.

And the sun was no furnace like the furnace in his head, roaring a flame-wind hurricane that deafened him for a moment, seeing Charlie and his scrawny hound in the front yard right out there by the fence, wrestling as if they were father and son, yelping at each other when each of them was younger; seeing Charlie outside Tucson a handful of years ago on his small, isolated ranch, riding a near white mare, pointing out the dozens, maybe hundreds of different cactuses that grew in the desert and laughing when a root that was a snake had made Jim yelp and twist so hard he nearly fell from the saddle; seeing Charlie at the Tennessee State Fair only last year, watching the girls watching him and shaking his head slowly because none that he wanted would want him if they knew.

Seeing Charlie and his shotgun.

Seeing the fire.

Seeing the bodies fall.

Bad news?"

He swallowed, and nodded, and swallowed again and said, "Look, would you mind putting off going for a bit? There's some things I have to do." He looked at her then. "A friend is dead. I have to do . . . things."

He could see she wanted to be sorry, and probably was in an abstract, he-was-a-stranger-to-me way.

While she waited on the porch—her choice, not his— he called the Chattanooga morgue and after arguing with several clerks and huffy bureaucrats arranged for Charlie's body to be brought to Potar Junction, once the police were finished. Arizona was home, but Charlie had no real family, and this was about as home as the fool would have gotten had he been able to have one. There were more questions, and a firmly polite refusal to drive down there himself.

He knew what Charlie looked like now, and it wouldn't fit the memory he expected to carry.

Charlie Acres would be partly skinned, and parts of him would be missing.

He called Rye Harden in town, told the undertaker what to expect, and where to send the bills. He barely tolerated the professional commiseration, and the none-too-subtle probing not at all.

"Just do it, Rye," and gave the man official names and dates given to him by the police.

When he hung up, he couldn't release the receiver, knuckles white, wrist quivering.

The hurricane blew.

Jesus, Charlie, Jesus, he thought as his fingers finally relaxed and, just for a moment, he pressed his forehead against the pane.

Then he was on the porch, taking the keys from Rachel's outstretched hand.

"You know," she said hesitantly, "I . . . I can always stay here, make myself something. It would keep me out of your hair. This, uh . . . I'm sorry about your friend. You probably want to be . . . you know."

He appreciated it, the words and the sentiment, and told her so.

Suddenly he sagged against the railing, gripped it in both hands, and lowered his head, closed his eyes. All energy was gone in a rush that surprised and unnerved him. It wasn't that something like this hadn't been expected; it happened all the time. But it wasn't supposed to happen to him and Charlie.

Cowboys and injuns, the man had once said; *Think of it as cowboys and injuns, if it'll make you feel better.*

Neither had reminded the other that the Indians sometimes won.

Gentle pressure on his back he recognized as her hand, and he took in the soft and hot, late afternoon air, first in gulps, then in sighs, until he was able to straighten and blink the sun from his eyes.

"Point of fact," he said, turning, feeling her hand glide around his waist until it fell away, "I could use some company about now. If you don't mind, that is."

"No, it's okay." Then her stomach gurgled, and her hand clamped over it. "Cost you that meal, though."

"You got it."

Into the car then, the windows down with the air conditioning blowing, and after backing out of the drive they headed north toward the tunnel of old trees.

"Where are we going?"

He drove with one hand; he didn't drive fast.

"A roadhouse up this way, just this side of the Junction. Good food. Clog your arteries. You'll love it." He didn't wear sunglasses, though the light was strong, and when he glanced at her he was squinting.

She didn't look back; she stared out the window, her left hand tracing patterns on her thigh.

Cattle lumbered in pastures, a clutch of wood beehives were shaded by a jutting fist of stone, a pair of buckskins chased each other across a rocky creek. And the horizon in every direction was sliced by mountains touched with haze.

Over a rise five slow curving miles from the house, gnarled, spotted-bark trees hovered at the shoulder for nearly half a mile, their high, overlacing boughs making it darker than he wanted it to be.

Once out the other side they exchanged tense smiles, and she asked him about Charlie, who he was, how he'd died. He almost didn't answer right away, not sure he could, finally told her Acres was a friend of long standing who had been killed by a drunk driver, hit-and-run, despite repeated warnings to stop hitchhiking at night.

"But he always did, the stupid bastard. Said it was the only way to travel."

"And it finally . . . killed him?"

"The dope."

He felt her stare and knew he'd made a mistake when he turned his head and saw her.

Those damn eyes had changed again, and it was there: *you're lying.*

How? he wondered; what did I say?

He lifted his foot from the accelerator and let the car drift toward the left shoulder. When he finally braked, they were midway along a whitewashed picket fence that marked a good fifteen acres of closely mown, rolling lawn touched with fruit trees and flowers. Three-quarters of the way back, on a low knoll at the foot of a paved drive, was an antebellum mansion tucked into a high-crowned stand of century oak. Down the road next to a counterbalanced gate was a scrolled sign hanging from black chains between two brass posts, but at the angle and the distance, he knew she couldn't read it.

She was confused. "This isn't . . . the roadhouse?"

He laughed softly. "Nope."

"Then why did we stop?"

He inhaled slowly, kept his right hand on the steering wheel, and used his left to gesture out the window.

"When I first came down here, about sixteen, seventeen years ago, I had this stupid idea of what it was supposed to be like to have . . . I don't know . . . money. I'd pretty much scrabbled for it most of my life, and I had built up a ton of notions about what rich people should have, the way they should behave, what they should wear, crap like that. So I built that place over there, Master of the Plantation.

"I had visions, by God. Lord, did I have visions.

"But since there was only me, you can see the place is too damn big, and I hate having people wait on me so there were no servants, and the next thing you know, I

was talking to myself." He laughed silently, pulled at his
nose, palm-brushed his hair. "Just li'l old me, if you can
imagine it, wandering from room to room, most of the
damn things empty, talking to myself. I felt like I was
living in some kind of echo chamber. And I damn well
knew I was driving myself nuts.

"Now the Master of the Plantation, especially when
he's from up North, he doesn't have many friends no
matter how many parties he throws. I learned damn quick
they have words for guys like me who come down here
with a suitcase full of money and a head full of notions.
'Carpetbagger' is about the most polite I heard.

"So after a while, it wasn't much more than a year, I
gave it up and built the other place."

"You're kidding. You actually gave this place away?"

"Yep."

"You must be nuts."

"Maybe." He wiped his forehead, and dried his palm
on his leg, where he left his hand, the fingers drumming
silently. "But amazingly enough, that's about when the
local folks started talking to me."

As they passed the mansion, at a near crawl so she could
see it all better, she read the elaborately detailed sign
aloud: "The Third Church of Jesus Christ? I never heard
of it."

"It's Maurice's," he explained, chuckling, and pointed
to a gleaming brass cross erected on the front porch. "The
guy I told you about, remember? From up on the Ridge?
The way he explains it, which he'll do at the drop of a
donation, the First Church is Heaven, the Second
Church is Hell because that's where the sinners are and
Jesus still wants to save them, only He's taking His sweet
time about it, so naturally, Maurice's place has to be the

Third." He tapped the steering wheel with his thumb. "Maurice has some interesting ideas about religion. Maybe you'll get to talk to him sometime."

"He's your friend, right?"

"Yeah, but he drives me crazy."

"Does he know Charlie?"

The answer was long coming. "Yep. A lot of years between those two."

"So shouldn't we go in and tell him? He should know, right? He's a friend."

Another glance; she was challenging him.

He looked away, puzzled and annoyed. "Don't worry about it. I'll tell him later. I need a little time, it's been too damn quick."

A hundred yards past the end of the picket fence, the road curved sharply down and to the right around a tall wide hill with a semi-circle pasture cleared midway up its slope; and beyond it, spread across a narrow valley, was a town.

"Potar Junction." He nodded at the two dozen or so buildings they could see, and to others hidden by trees and shadows and a vague drift of rising mist that blurred the valley's far end. "Farmers and small business mostly, some lumber people, and a couple of outlet things on another road you can't make out from here that bring in some bucks. You probably passed the signs on the interstate. There are lots of small places like this back here, you just can't see them, which most of them figure is all right by them." He pointed to the right. "That there's Cider Dunn's place."

It was a long white building wanting a good scrubbing and fresh paint, with a partially graveled parking lot in front, a bar on one end, a restaurant on the other. A satellite dish took up most of a weedy side yard, and two rusted pickups lay beached and blocked in the other. He decided not to tell her any stories about the way the two establishments sometimes tended to collide on weekend nights; and if she concluded that the small house in back, pushed behind straggly trees, was where Cider lived, he wouldn't correct her. If Nola was working, Rachel would figure it out soon enough.

There was nothing subtle about Nola Paine.

After avoiding a pothole large enough to sink a wheel, he turned into the dirt-and-gravel lot and parked between a pickup and a new Mercedes, at the restaurant door; there were already half a dozen other vehicles settled down by the bar, and when he got out he could hear music blaring from the bar's screened windows.

Rachel didn't react one way or the other, at least not that he could tell. Not when she heard the music, and not when he muttered a curse as he yanked open the stuck screen door and gestured her in ahead of him. Not when she saw the dimly lighted room, and not when he brought her to a table against the left wall. In the back corner.

From the outside, Dunn's Place looked only two or three steps distant from a basic honky-tonk dive, and if she had gone into the other side, she wouldn't have been disappointed. Old bar, old pool table, scuffed flooring, and the smell of beer and fights and anticipated sex. The jukebox hadn't been dusted in five years, the tiny dance floor in back heel-scuffed and squeaky, and the two front windows had more dead bugs and grit than space to see through.

This half, however, would not have been out of place in a small, respectable hotel in a small, respectable city. The walls were wainscoted in dark pine, papered in old-fashioned flowers and vines above. Framed oils, polished floors, leather-padded chairs, lamps on the walls and chimney candles on the tables. A family of five sitting by the picture window near the entrance, two men in jeans and plaid shirts sitting in the center, each holding a cup of coffee. It was so heavily soundproofed that the bar's pounding music was only a barely felt vibration, easily ignored, easily forgotten.

A waitress in flats, and a uniform that could have passed for a nurse's, save for the pearl buttons down the front, and showy lace at collar and abundant bodice, dropped two large plastic menus on the table and poured them each a tumbler of water. "Evening, Jimmy."

He smiled up at her. "Hey, Nola, how you doing?"

Nola Paine grinned. She was tall, but not slender, and her hair had been brushed back into a ponytail with a loop. "Better and better." She glanced at Rachel, who nodded a greeting. "Could be worse."

"I doubt it," he said.

She winked at him and moved over to the family by the window.

Rachel did turn then, watching the waitress' stiff awkward stride; then she looked back at him. "She did that deliberately, didn't she. Because of me."

Jim smiled, somehow not surprised. "Yeah, guess so. Usually those hips knock over a couple of tables, put a dent in the walls. I've known men who've gotten seasick just watching her go out to her car."

"The Mercedes."

His eyebrow cocked.

Her answering smile was unsure.

He pointed at her menu.

"Hey," she said, leaning toward him, lowering her voice, "are you sure this is all right? I mean, with your—"

A raised finger stopped her. "Look, it's going to sound pretty corny, all right? but Charlie would've wanted it like this. The truth be known, he'd probably prefer I just get damn drunk."

"Okay," she said, still uncertain but willing to go along.

More patrons arrived, the noise level rose, and sunlight turned to twilight, in turn transforming the window family into nodding silhouettes.

When the dinners were served, Rachel gave Nola a genuine smile, and he could sense the waitress trying to decide just how to handle this, how she should behave. It amused him, but he didn't smile, and finally Rachel, after pooling some ketchup beside her steak, an act that made him cringe, stabbed her knife over her shoulder. "Nice car."

Nola grunted and stood beside him, cocking a hip by his shoulder, not quite touching but close enough to feel. "Honey, it would be if the son of a bitch worked once in a while. Guy I bought it from, he's from down near Cleveland? he swears I don't drive it right, but shit, if you don't want to fly, why buy a plane?"

He looked up; Nola winked at him again. Broadly.

"Kin?" she asked, no innocence at all.

"Not hardly," Rachel answered for him. Dryly. "Friend."

The waitress laughed, reached out and shook her hand.

"Listen, honey, you come by next door when you're done, I'll fix you a drink on the house."

"You work there too?"

Nola laughed loudly, but no one seemed to notice.

Jim did, and it made him uncertain. Then he glanced up and realized Rachel was trying to wipe a blush from her cheeks.

"Sorry," she muttered.

"Hell, that's all right," the waitress said. She leaned over, looked at each of them in turn. "Listen, I got half the mad dogs in this county sniffing around this place, so I'm glad there's going to be one less of them for a while."

Jim choked.

Rachel laughed.

"Besides," Nola continued, "if Jim here wasn't trying so damn hard to ignore me, I'd think I was losing it." She made a quick, look-but-don't-look, gesture to the table in the middle. "Those two boys now, they've been sitting there for an hour and all they want is damn coffee. I tell them they can get that in the bar and not take up air and space, and all they do is lift their cups. You think they're on one of them California diets or something?" She straightened, and smoothed her skirt when a customer called her name. "Eat," she ordered. "You'll need your strength."

Rachel laughed again, blushed again, and Jim did his best not to strangle the woman. He had known Nola Paine for over a decade, and though he'd been to her house, and she to his, more times than he could remember, he also counted her a friend. A damn close friend. Whenever he got an idea on how to spend his money, she loaded him up with common sense and sent him home; whenever he drank too much and wept openly about his sister, she hushed him, and undressed him, and tucked him into bed.

He closed his eyes briefly.

That was going to be the bitch—telling Rachel about Maryanne.

He hoped he wouldn't have to do it.

He hoped he wouldn't have to drink in order to do it.

"Nice lady," Rachel said into the silence.

He gave her a sour stare. "Yeah, when she ain't flapping her lips off."

Then something ticked over, something Nola had said, and he glanced at the two men she'd talked about, the ones he'd seen when he and Rachel had come in.

At the same time, one of them looked at him.

Smiled broadly, but swiftly.

And raised his cup in a silent mocking toast.

Oh shit, Jim thought; oh shit.

T he two men rose, noisily scraping their chairs back. One was tall and lank, his face long, and his eyes long and narrow beneath a shock of hair that dangled over his brow; the other was shorter, but not by much, and heavier, by a lot. They picked up battered and stained western hats from the empty chairs at their table, put them on, hid their eyes, and walked out of the restaurant without looking at anyone.

Their dusty boots were loud and harsh on the bare floor, louder on the boardwalk that led to the bar.

Jim swallowed.

"What is it?"

It took him several moments before he could see her clearly.

"Jim, are you all right?"

The family at the window rose, chattering and shifting, passing in and out of what was left of the light, their voices mingling into a sing-song hum.

Beyond them, in the twilight dragging over the valley, he saw an automobile pull slowly out of the parking lot, and stop on the road, engine running.

Rachel was right.

The Caddy looked like a boat.

J im didn't realize he was half out of his seat until Rachel reached across the table and put a hand over his.

"What's wrong?"

She turned as he lowered himself again, turned just as the huge Cadillac passed out of sight.

The fork dropped unnoticed from her fingers, and she nearly stood herself until her hand caught the edge of the table and held her. Barely held her.

He said nothing.

When she twisted back around, her face was drawn and pale, and suddenly those eyes were disturbingly dark. "It was them," she whispered angrily, and was on her feet before he could move to stop her, her napkin flung onto her plate. "Let's go."

"Where?"

"To get them, you shit. They were here, and you didn't stop them. What the hell's the matter with you?"

She was halfway across the room before he could think to follow, and already out the door by the time he'd managed to fumble some bills from his pocket and drop them on the table. When he reached the parking lot, she was on the shoulder, shading her eyes as she looked south, a haze of dust hanging over the blacktop. Then she marched back to the car, got in, slammed the door, and glared at him through the windshield until he joined her.

From inside the bar someone played a blues guitar.

"Bastard," she whispered.

He started the engine.

"You goddamn bastard."

He saw his eyes in the rearview mirror as he backed out of his slot, couldn't meet the look, and looked away.

She growled deep in her throat, and punched his arm. Once. Very hard. "They were going to kill me, you son of a bitch, they were going to kill me."

Go ahead; tell her.

"Who are they, Scott, friends of yours? Good ol' boys from good ol' Potar Junction? Don't rock the fucking boat, you'll ruin your precious little hillbilly kingdom? Is that it, huh? Is that it?"

He didn't look; he could hear the tears in every word.

"You son of a bitch."

The sun had set, the mountains and hills pulling back into the dark.

There were no streetlights, only the headlamps that turned the blacktop grey.

"Christ, you're probably one of them."

He braked so hard she nearly slammed into the dashboard.

He didn't turn his head.

"I am not one of them," he said quietly, though it seemed as if he were shouting. Then he did face her, and was not moved by the way she shrank against the door. He knew what he looked like. He knew how he sounded. "Say it again, lady, you can walk the hell back to Virginia."

Her lips trembled; she didn't speak; her left hand quivered, and pushed at the air, *drive on, drive on, for God's sake, drive on.*

He did.

And when he reached the entrance to the Third

Church of Jesus Christ, he swerved sharply into the drive-way without touching the brakes and sped toward the house, ignoring her angry questions as he took a narrower blacktop drive around to the right and parked in front of the veranda. Huge redwood tubs at each of the six pillars held well-tended shrubs, and flanking the high double doors similar tubs each held a small palm tree whose fronds were thin and limp.

Maurice Lion, in a white suit and white plantation hat, sat in a white wicker chair and held a tall glass in his hand. Behind him stood two young women in billowing white robes, their skin much darker than his, their hair in plaits curled atop their heads.

Jim got out without speaking, without looking to see if Rachel would follow. He followed an inlaid brick path to the steps and nodded to himself when he heard Rachel's door slam. But he really didn't care. She came, she didn't come, he didn't give a damn. Not now.

"Maurice," he said.

The preacher showed his teeth. "James. Welcome." Then he waved to Rachel and bade her join him with a grandiose gesture. "And young lady, welcome as well. I do hope you are enjoying your stay in our country."

She glanced at Jim, anger shifting awkwardly to confusion.

He touched her arm and followed her up the steps. "He means God's country. We're all visitors here."

"You learn well, my friend."

"You say it long enough, I'm going to remember it whether I want to or not."

Maurice's laugh came in short bursts, each burst a note, each series a chorus. Had the mountains been closer, they would have echoed into a choir. Then he stood and swept off his hat, and Rachel took an involuntary step back. He was tall, the preacher was, and though he'd never given a measurement, Jim guessed him to be damn close to seven feet. He was also completely bald. Though clearly black, his skin was light, and as he brushed the air over a chair for Rachel, his long fingers flowed, his lips moving in a murmur until her comfort was assured. A snap of his fingers, and the two women glided into the house, closing the doors behind them without a sound.

"My angels," he explained as he retook his own seat.

"Reverend, I . . ." Rachel blinked several times in confusion. "Jim . . ." She gave up.

Jim understood. It had taken him years to get hold of the man; he was forever dancing, forever a shadow, now you see him, now you don't, and it was no wonder the people around here, black and white, either feared him, or laughed at him, or would march to the sea on razor blades for him.

He leaned a shoulder against one of the posts, a thumb tucked behind his buckle. Above his head, and at intervals along the veranda, electric insect grids glowed faintly. Globed lamps hung from chains, but they remained unlit. There was only the glow from the tall windows that faced the yard, and that was dim enough.

Maurice leaned forward, hands clasping his knees. "Child, you seem worried." He looked at Jim. "Is she troubled? Has she need?"

"She—"

"I was attacked the other night, Reverend," Rachel said bluntly. "Someone chased me off the road up on that ridge where you wanted to put the cross. Jim told me about it after I managed to make it to his place."

Maurice straightened. "The police?"

"I . . . we didn't call them."

"James." A chiding, a question, a demand.

Jim wiped his face with the back of his free hand.

"He knows who they are," she accused bitterly. "We just saw them at that restaurant back there, and he didn't try to stop them."

"I couldn't," he said to the preacher. "I wasn't sure until it was too late."

Rachel snorted.

An insect died in a buzzing explosion.

Maurice leaned back and crossed his legs. He wore no socks, no tie, his shirt was open to the center of his chest. Then his eyes half closed, his fingers tenting beneath his chin.

"Ah," he said, and drew out the sound until it came close to sighing.

"God!" Rachel shouted. "Jesus Christ!"

"Indeed," said Maurice with a quick nod. "For the Lord has placed His beloved creatures every one upon His Earth for every reason. Some to kill and some to feed and some to carry beauty and some to remind others that beauty can be deadly. Isn't that right, James? Is that not His purpose?" He answered himself with another short sharp nod. "And the Lord created us all, and Man to hold dominion. It is said, child, that nothing is wasted which cannot be used, and nothing that cannot be used shall be wasted, for it is sinful."

"For crying out loud, Maurice," Jim muttered impatiently. What he didn't need now was one of the man's impromptu sermons.

"What the hell does that mean?" Rachel snapped.

Maurice blinked.

Jim shifted to face her. "What it means is that he knows them too."

Her eyes widened, her lips moved in an attempt to speak which she gave up when she could find neither the words nor the emotion. Instead, she slapped to her feet and demanded to be taken to the authorities in Potar Junction, or wherever the hell they were.

Jim couldn't argue, and cut Maurice's answer off with an upheld palm. "Not now," he told him. "Not now."

The preacher didn't protest. He picked up his glass and sipped, picked up an empty glass and offered to pour Rachel a share from the pitcher on the table beside him. She refused. He sipped again.

Jim cleared his throat, turning her face to him. "You asked me what I did."

"Yes," she said. "And you told me you didn't do anything, you were rich."

"I lied," he told her, and added quickly, "Well, not quite a lie. I am rich, that's the truth. It's just that what I do doesn't go on very often."

"Oh brother," she said disgustedly. She started for the car. "Take me to the police. Now."

He grabbed her arm, and didn't try again when she smacked his hand away.

"Give me the keys," she demanded, facing him squarely. "Give me the goddamn keys."

He didn't move.

She appealed to the preacher with a trembling right hand.

Jim said, "Remember the other night?"

She froze.

"They're out there again."

Her breathing turned to shudders.

"And that's what I do, Rachel. When I can, I hunt the jackals."

adness is what it was, and the strength of it made her weak.

She refused to look at either of them, but when she stepped nervously away from the house and saw the stars, saw the moon, she couldn't look there either. Her hands flapped uselessly at her sides, fingers searching for a grip on something, finally raking into her hair and down across her chest.

They were watching her.

With a deliberate turn of her head, she tried to find something peaceful, something comforting about the vast sweep of lawn that reached back to the fence, about the barn she spotted back there in the far corner and the recognition of a pungent smell, a barnyard, that wrinkled her nose though it wasn't unpleasant.

Madness; it was madness.

She swallowed a sob, because it would have turned to laughter.

Then she heard the preacher say, "They were there, James? In Cider's den?"

"Christ Almighty, not you, too."

"It's a fair question, don't you think?"

Angrily Jim pushed away from the pillar. "No, goddamnit. No, I do not think it's a fair question. How was I supposed to recognize them, huh? Give me a hint, Maurice, give me a fucking hint." He took a breath. "You think they carry goddamn name tags? Hello, my name is whatever the hell they call themselves these days? You think they carry signs?"

In three steps he was across the veranda and leaning over the cleric. Rachel saw his hands grab the armrests, how his arms trembled not to throw a punch, how the preacher merely lifted his hat's brim so he could see his friend's eyes.

"I am not one of your almighty prophets, Maurice." His voice was low again, rough again, and when he lifted a finger to point it at the preacher, the preacher flinched. "I am not a goddamn superman."

Rachel flinched as well; she had seen the fear, there and gone, in Lion's eyes.

This man was more, much more than she'd believed.

The two men glared at each other for several unbearable seconds before Jim shoved himself upright and spun toward her. His face was in shadow, all the light behind him. Taller, somehow. Larger. Hair turned to harsh white fire.

"I didn't know."

It wasn't an excuse. It wasn't a plea for reason.

It just was, nothing more.

She didn't respond. A dizzying weariness threatened to fell her because there had been too many swings from hope to confusion to anger and back. Each time she thought she'd reached solid ground, a shadow became a hole, and she was tired of not quite falling in.

Momma always told her, don't bite off more than she could chew.

It had sounded stupid all her life; not so stupid now.

"James," Lion said quietly, "she came to your house."

"Tell me something I don't know."

Jim looked at her, but she knew, with a chill, that he didn't really see her.

"James, did you hear me?"

Her head jerked left. Something flared up on the road. "James?"

Jim came off the steps in a slow hurry, and she backed away, out of reach of the light, as he walked far enough into the yard to be able to see for himself what she had spotted—three pair of headlamps shooting around the curve out of the valley, and finally the sound of three racing engines bouncing off the hill on the far side of the road.

With an unnecessary motion for her to stay where she was, he moved quickly to his right, to see around the other side of the house as the headlamps became taillights that rose and fell with the land before winking out in the tunnel of trees.

He watched.

She watched with him.

The cars didn't return.

She moved up behind him. "I don't get it. Why do you call them jackals?"

"It is the way the Lord made all His creatures," Lion answered from the veranda. "There are those who hunt, and those who are hunted." He took off his hat with a flourish and balanced it on his knee. "And there are those who are ordained to sweep behind the armies and clear the land of the fallen, the injured, those who cannot carry the Lord's Word any longer. It is written in—"

"Maurice," said Jim wearily, "will you shut the hell up?"

"I only speak the Lord's Will."

"Try speaking when spoken to."

Lion rose smoothly to his feet, and swept on his hat. "I will forgive you, James, because, God knows, you need forgiveness."

"The hell with me, use it on Charlie. He's dead."

The preacher closed his eyes.

Jim rubbed his face with a palm, drew the hand stiffly down his chest. "Well, damn you, Maurice, I didn't want to tell you that way." He threw a false punch at one of the pillars. "Damnit."

A soft keening note slipped into the air.

"Not now, Maurice," he said. "Please. Not now."

"I mourn," the deep voice answered.

"Mourn tomorrow. They're here tonight."

Rachel decided that in some cartoon Wonderland-like way, their madness was comforting. Had she herself been truly sane, she would have found a way to kill both these two an hour ago. And that certainly wouldn't have done her much good, certainly wouldn't have saved her.

Maurice strode to the edge of the veranda and looked south along the unseen road. He shaded his eyes. He stretched out his left arm as though he were a pointer. He turned on one foot and pointed at her.

"You went to his house."

"I—"

"Don't tell me, child. You went to his house."

Rather than argue, she ignored him. Instead she touched Jim's arm until he faced her. "He was talking about scavengers, wasn't he. Like crows and things. Carrion eaters, animals like that."

Jim nodded.

She frowned. "But what does that—"

Headlamps flared again, this time through the tunnel

trees, distracting her once more. It wasn't until the lights had broken into the open and the car had slowed that she realized something was wrong.

"Jim," she said.

Another insect died.

He looked at the passing vehicle, shrugged, but she said it again when the car disappeared as the mansion came between them: "Jim."

"What? It's just—"

"The engine. I can't hear the engine."

Maurice didn't have to rush to reach the double doors in a hurry. He opened one and stepped inside. Directly ahead was the rear wall of a sweeping black oak staircase that led to the second-story gallery. The wall had ten inlaid panels carved with leaves of ivy, and when he had complained at the wasted space, Jim had shown him that if he used the heel of his hand to whack the left side of the three center panels, each would open into a fair-size long closet.

He smacked the first one on the right just as his angels came around the corner.

"I think you'd better go to your rooms, pack, go home to your mommas," he said as he reached in and flicked on a light. "I may be gone for a while."

He smiled at them, touched their cheeks. "And be sure the front doors are locked and bolted before you go upstairs. Turn out all the lights."

They turned and walked away.

Lord, he thought, plucking a shotgun from its rack, I am too old for this now.

A rifle from another rack, its scope still attached.

O Lord, I have done my best, You know. I am not a perfect man, but I'm as close as they're going to get in this forsaken county, You know that. Don't You think I deserve something better than this?

He remembered the first time he had entered this small room; it was the day after his first angel had been found

on the highway. What was left of her. And the second
time . . . oh lord, he thought, and tried to banish that
image, the one that showed him that Jim had finally
found Maryanne.

What was left of her.

A spurt of bile made him touch his stomach with one
hand, knead it, pat it; and he swallowed, took a breath,
and suggested to his shadow spread across the bare floor
that this was no time to wallow in memories best left for
bad dreams.

The bile surged again, and subsided.

From a high walnut cabinet against the back wall he
grabbed several boxes of ammunition and stuffed them
into his pockets. He considered another rifle for the
woman, but he didn't believe she was the shooting kind.
A revolver then, small enough for her to handle and large
enough to do the job. He loaded it for her and prayed
there was enough time to show her how to use it.

And, Lord, he added as he checked the room again,
take care of Charlie's soul. He was a good man. He was
too young. He didn't deserve it.

"Damn, Maurice, we're not going to start a war."

He glanced over his shoulder, at Jim standing in the
doorway, one hand half in a hip pocket. "If this isn't a
war, I'd much prefer to be in bed." He tossed the rifle to
his friend, followed it with the gun. "Are they coming?"

"Rachel's looking out. I don't think so, though."

"Neither, my friend, did you think they'd be back."

Jim looked everywhere but at him. "Charlie told me
. . . he called last night, this morning, I don't know. He
was at a pay phone outside some diner, said he spotted
them down around Birmingham."

"Them?"

"The Modeens."

"Oh mercy."

"All of them. He said, as far as he could tell, it was pretty much all of them."

Maurice wished he had a place to sit down.

"He tried to tell me something else, too, but he never had the chance." Jim stared at the barrel. "He got cut off." He looked up at Maurice. "They found him outside Chattanooga, just like . . . like . . ."

He managed a cockeyed bitter smile.

In that moment, quick enough for a blink, Maurice wondered how his friend survived when there wasn't hunting to do.

He wondered what would happen when all the hunting was over.

"Do you know what it was, James, the information? Can you guess?"

Jim rubbed the rifle's stock absently. "It's been ten years," he said at last, quietly, as if afraid the house would overhear. "He could have meant she's there too."

"And you waited until now to tell me?" Maurice raised a hand to point, to scold, and let it fall helplessly to his side; what's the use, it's too late now. "They let Charlie be found, they let the child out there go to your home. What in the name of heaven are you thinking of, James?"

Jim didn't answer; he only stared, then walked away.

Lord, I am cursed with a fluent tongue and a big mouth. Can't You see Your way clear to heal me of one or the other?

He looked around again, just in case he'd missed something, then slapped off the light and closed the panel door. By the time he reached the veranda, Jim was at the car, rifle loose at his side. There was no signal, just a look, and he allowed himself a deep breath and quick prayer to calm his nerves and disperse the tension.

The woman stood behind a tall evergreen shrub at the corner of the house, the revolver in one hand. When she glanced at him, no emotion at all, he nodded his approval. With the moon this bright, and no houselight in her eyes, she could see the length of the drive and a good portion of the road. He reminded himself to ask James about her later as he crossed to the man's side.

"Left?"

Jim shook his head. "No, don't think so."

Rachel waved at them to hush.

The night was too quiet.

Maurice scowled briefly, tilted his head, straining, before he realized what was wrong—the insects had stopped talking, the breeze had died, and all he could hear was his own shallow breathing, steady and calm. He wasn't afraid. The time would come, but it wasn't now.

They heard it then: a soft whistle, long and slow and mournful.

And then, in the dark beyond the house, in the shadows of the moon, they heard the laughter.

As the woman scuttled away from the shrub toward the safety of the house, Maurice jacked a round into its chamber and hurried to the right corner, swallowed, and allowed himself to slip off the veranda into the shadows. There was a flower bed here but no flowers, the six-foot-wide strip of earth kept constantly tilled, constantly soft.

He called it his moat, the house on one side and a low wall of shrubs on the other, and James had laughed when Maurice had made it, but it served him now, dampening the sound of his progress toward the front while the laughter ended, hanging beneath the stars, neither tempting nor daring.

Yet he still wasn't afraid.

Had the Modeens meant real business, there'd be more than just the two, and they wouldn't have come in from the road, it was too open.

Not afraid, but sudden perspiration washed over his face, slipped down his spine.

At the front corner he pressed hard against the house and used the moon to show him the upward slope of the lawn, the trees, the circle gardens, the road.

He saw the car and heard it idling softly, the low rumble of a large cat patient and hungry; he wished for something to moisten his throat—it felt as if it had been packed with raw cotton—he couldn't swallow, and fought to keep himself from coughing to clear it.

He didn't see them.

They were out there, he knew it; he could feel them, but he couldn't see them.

He crouched halfway to kneeling and allowed himself a quick glance around the corner, across the length of the front porch. It was empty, all the lights extinguished, the brass cross he'd fixed into the floor the day he'd moved in shimmering faintly, darkly, barely touched by the moon.

He waited.

There was nothing else to do.

He waited.

Watching the gardens for unlikely shadows, watching

the fruit trees for an extra thickness of bole, using the
idling engine up there on the shoulder to keep him alert,
to remind him this wasn't a dream, they had come.

He didn't ask himself why.

And he didn't think twice when he saw the shadow
move.

It slipped away from a pear tree halfway to the road,
slipped across the silver grass sea, heading for the fence,
moving smoothly, moving swiftly, in a straight line for
the car.

Maurice fired.

Too far for damage, but it didn't matter.

He fired again and grinned, all his teeth showing, at the
sound that slammed back from the hill across the way.

Stepped away from the house and fired a third time
when the shadow stopped and turned to face him.

After grabbing a long-butt flashlight from the car's back seat, Jim slipped along the left side of the house, scowling when Rachel insisted on going with him, puzzling him as she appeared to know what she was doing, keeping low, keeping tight to the wall, keeping the revolver aimed at the sky. Either too much TV, or there was something here she hadn't told him.

He figured Maurice would go straight to the corner to watch the lawn and the drive; he would do the same, and at the same time hope to catch them in case they came from the north. He doubted that, however, because it was too open, no cover unless they had learned to merge with the low-cut grass; but he had doubted before, on other occasions, and hadn't yet been able to anticipate surprise.

At the corner he dropped to one knee, rifle ready, breathing steady.

Nothing out there.

The Caddy was on the shoulder, but there were too many damn gardens, too many damn trees, for him to know for sure which was real and which was one of them.

He could hear Rachel breathing carefully behind him through her mouth.

He didn't look back.

He watched the still shadows, taking care not to look at any one for too long.

What the hell were they up to? he wondered, nearly

trembling in the effort to keep his anger under control; what the hell were they doing?

He shifted, keeping the flashlight in his left hand, holding the rifle in his right.

Rachel made a sound deep in her throat and pointed over his shoulder.

A shadow moved.

The shotgun blasted.

Jim broke immediately from the house's cover and ran for the drive, dropping the flashlight as he did to use both hands on the rifle, wincing when the shotgun fired again, stopping when the shadow did, sensing Maurice leave his place as well and bracing himself for the next blast of fire.

It came.

The shadow waved and walked calmly toward the fence.

Jim ran a few steps, put the stock to his shoulder and caught the shadow, still a shadow, in the cross-hairs of his scope.

Rachel came up beside him.

He fired, and the top of a post blew apart.

The shadow laughed and vaulted the fence, ran around to the car's far side as Jim fired twice more, the Caddy jumping slightly on its springs as the bullets slammed into the door.

The engine roared.

The shadow ducked down as if to get inside, then took a moment to look over the roof at the two men and the woman racing toward it.

Jim glanced at Rachel, saw the flashlight in her free hand, and said, "Turn it on!"

She didn't move.

He said, "Turn the damn light on!" and fired this time without bothering to aim.

Maurice saw the light, saw the face transfixed, saw what he knew he'd see, and still he turned away.

Rachel knew she held a gun, but she couldn't bring herself to raise it.

My God, she thought, my God. Why hadn't she left when she had the chance? Why the hell had she stayed?

She paid no attention to the face that quickly vanished when the shadow ducked into the car; she didn't move when Jim began a loping angled run up the drive, firing as he went, but clearly without hope of preventing the car's escape; she didn't move when Maurice stomped across the porch and told her she might as well save the batteries, they were gone, it was over.

She stared at the flashlight, switched it off, and dropped it.

"When you drive at night," the preacher said, coming slowly to her side, "you catch a deer, a possum, a raccoon in your lights, sometimes a stray tom on his way to see his lady. I've seen them red, those eyes, once in a while green, once in a while a pale yellow, maybe gold. The first time I saw that . . ."

Suddenly she grabbed the flashlight from the ground and shone it in the preacher's face. He didn't flinch, he smiled sadly, and she aimed the beam at the grass.

She was right—his eyes didn't reflect the way an animal's would.

But the man on the road.

His eyes glowed.

They glowed white.

Suddenly, Jim raced past her, shouted to Maurice, "Peter!", and tossed something at her chest. She caught it, the car keys, and heard him tell her to get the engine going, he'd be back in a minute.

She didn't hesitate, but ran for the car, suddenly sagged against the door. She wasn't sure she could do this. It was happening much too fast.

Maurice took the keys gently. "It's all right," he said. "Get in back."

She gave him a grateful weak smile and climbed in, huddling in the corner behind the passenger seat while the preacher turned the car around. Nausea surged and died in her stomach. She breathed with her mouth open to keep the dizziness at bay. Then Jim was back. Maurice sped to the road, fishtailed as he turned south, nearly putting them into the shallow ditch on the other side.

She closed her eyes, lower lip trembling as much from fear of the men in front as the men in the car they chased through the night.

When they reached the tree tunnel, she realized her

right hand was near to cramping, stared at it, and saw the gun still in her grip.

"Peter'll put something on the road," Jim said tightly.

Maurice nodded.

"Did you tell him to keep Jonelle home?"

The preacher nodded again.

Moonlight helped, but not that much.

Rachel could barely see beyond the reach of the headlamps, and what she could see were merely blurs of grey.

The road ahead was empty.

"Maybe they turned off," she said, hating the sound of her very small voice.

"No." Jim gestured vaguely. "Nothing between here and there but the interstate."

"And an old farm," Maurice said. "Moore's place, the old man that moved to Phoenix."

"Right. Yeah, right."

They slowed for a moment when they reached Jim's house, and he leaned intently toward it, staring, before Maurice drove on, as fast as the curves and climbs would allow.

"The Snake," Jim said then.

Maurice grunted.

"What?" Rachel didn't like the way her voice sounded.

"A curve," Jim explained. He used one hand, illuminated by the dash, to illustrate. "The Ridge—where they had you?—it sweeps back from the interstate, pretty rocky and steep on this side, you went down the other. On the back side, facing us, the road follows it in an S-curve, a really sharp S-curve. If we don't get them before, they'll have to slow down then."

Rachel wanted to ask another question, a dozen more,

but she was afraid to speak again. This wasn't madness anymore; this was nightmare, and she was wide awake, wishing it was a dream.

She shuddered.

Too late now.

All she had to do was keep control.

Then Jim said, "There," and she sat up.

Red lights in the distance, close to the ground.

Suddenly they flared, and Jim said, "Peter."

Rachel," Maurice said as the car slowed quickly, "best you stay in here, child."

She nodded mutely.

Ahead, as the car stopped, she could see the back of the Caddy but nothing inside, no one on the road. A steep wooded slope rose sharply on the left, and the moon showed her what might have been a broad field on the right.

Jim opened his door, rifle in hand, moving so slowly he didn't seem to be moving at all.

Despite a silent warning to stay hidden in the shadow, she shifted forward, watching, thinking maybe she could help anyway by spotting some movement the others hadn't.

With the door open, she could hear the rumble of the Caddy's engine.

With the door open, she could hear nothing else but the night.

Maurice slid out, shotgun against his chest.

Twenty yards beyond the white Cadillac headlamps flared, and Rachel winced, nearly ducked, but the two men didn't move; she assumed that was Peter, whoever he was, blocking the road.

Were they there, she wondered, straining to see movement inside the white car. Unless they had jumped out while the Caddy was still moving, they hadn't had the time. They had to be there, but she could see through the rear window and saw no one, not a thing.

Jim and Maurice still hadn't moved.

The engine rumbled.

Her eyes began to burn from staring too long. She rubbed them quickly with the back of one hand, and didn't say a word when Jim whispered to her, "Watch," and stepped around his open door, rifle at the ready.

She checked out the back and saw nothing but black; it was no use trying to spot anything beyond the shoulders; she could only watch as the two men approached the white car, one cautious step at a time. She had no idea how many others were in Peter's car, but she assumed they were doing the same thing.

The engine rumbled.

She felt herself shaking and pressed against the back of Jim's seat, gripping it with her free hand until her fingers ached. She licked her lips. She swallowed. She almost cried out when, as the two men were midway between Jim's car and the Caddy, the Caddy's engine suddenly bellowed, whined, rear tires spinning and smoking for purchase on the blacktop.

There was no time to duck.

Gunshots and fire.

The Caddy lurched side to side, not getting far at all before it dove nose first into the ditch on the right.

Without thinking, she pushed the seat forward and scrambled out while Jim and Maurice walked forward, slowly. She could see no marks on the white vehicle's surface, but the tires she could see were shredded.

The passenger door swung open.

Jim stopped.

Maurice moved on, angling toward the far shoulder.

A dark figure split the headlamps of Peter's car.

The engine died.

She heard the laughter.

Soft, and mocking, more than one, more than two.

There was a woman in there.

Oh God, she thought, grabbing the doorframe to hold herself up. Her legs felt weak, the gun too heavy.

A man slipped awkwardly out of the white car, fell to one knee on the slope and shook his head, long hair slapping his arms as he pulled himself upright.

She held her breath.

She heard the laughter, and saw movement inside.

Creaking metal told her another door had opened.

The man tried to stand normally, but the slope defeated him and he leaned back against the door, legs wide and braced. His face was gaunt and unshaven, his body lean. He gripped the top of the door.

He smiled.

Rachel froze.

"I see the fawn," he said, looking straight at her.

A dark figure settled in the doorway, but she couldn't see more than a blond head, a plaid shirt.

He looked at Jim. "You ruined my car."

Jim didn't answer.

The creak of the driver's door opening.

"Don't, lady!" she heard a man's voice warn from somewhere down the road.

"Stay put," the standing man said calmly.

Rachel wanted to see where Maurice had gone, but she didn't want to move her head, barely dared to breathe. But she couldn't help thinking that this was the man who had pushed her over the Ridge; this man, or someone else in there, was the one who had nearly killed her.

The man took a slow breath. "Now what, Scott?"

The firing began.

Someone on the other side darted into the light, and was slammed to the ground by a shotgun's blast. By the time Rachel's startled scream escaped, there were more guns, glass shattering, the standing man on his hands and knees and toppling, the blond falling headfirst into the ditch, his legs still inside.

It didn't last very long.

And when it was over, acrid smoke curled and hovered in the headlights and the moonlight.

Rachel sat heavily on the ground, looked at her hand, grimaced, and tossed the gun into the car. She watched

Jim approach the Caddy, the bodies, rifle down at his side. Maurice stepped into the light from the far side, and the other man, Peter, joined him. They shook hands, solemnly; a meeting, not congratulations.

Jim stepped over the dead man on the slope and peered into the car. He straightened. "Four," he said, no inflection in his voice.

Four, Rachel thought numbly; four.

It seemed like more.

Maurice and Peter joined him as he walked around the trunk. Peter was not quite as tall as Jim, dark hair and dark mustache, his legs thick in tight jeans. They spoke quietly, just the sounds not the words reaching Rachel as she hauled herself to her feet, swayed, and grabbed the door.

Jim saw her.

She shook her head: *stay away, please stay away.*

He beckoned.

She shook her head again.

The smoke was gone, but the smell of gunpowder remained.

Jim handed his weapon to Peter and started over, and even in the car lights' glare, she could see the lines and the weariness in his face, in his eyes. He stumbled once, recovered, and gave her a sickly grin.

He stayed by the front bumper. "You're in shock," he said simply.

She found her voice: "Shock?" She pointed at the bodies, unable to stop the shaking. "I'm an accomplice, for Christ's sake! You murdered them!"

He glanced over his shoulder. "In an hour none of this will be here. Less. You're an accomplice to nothing."

She wanted to sit again. She swung herself around and dropped onto the front seat, lowering her head, clasping her quaking hands between her thighs. She heard him come around the car, felt him hunker down in front of her, heard him breathing, felt him watching.

"Modeens," he said softly.

She couldn't look, but her attitude said, *you killed them*.

The sound of a car's engine and, oddly, a truck's.

She didn't look, not even when she was sure she heard a woman's voice.

I will not pass out, she ordered, and stared at the road, at one small pebble poking out of the tarmac, until her eyes began to water; I will not pass out.

I will not cry.

Footsteps and grinding gears.

Without moving her head, she met Jim's gaze. "I didn't think you'd . . . he didn't have a gun or anything." It was a plea more than an accusation. "He just stood there."

The sound of a winch, of groaning metal; whispered voices.

"Rachel," he said at last, "let me tell you about the jackals."

They ride mostly with the night.

I've never believed, not after what I've seen these past few years, that people are really all that much different than animals. Call it God's plan, call it evolution, I don't know and I don't care, there are animals out here and they live in houses instead of dens and they like to pretend they're not the same as their pets or the things they see in their zoos or on TV or in the movies.

Maybe they aren't.

Maybe they are.

But some of them ride mostly with the night.

On your way here, Rachel, you saw it more than once, I know you did—those cars on the side of the road, late at night, white cloth hanging from a door handle or a window, signaling for help from the cops or a passing trucker.

Maybe they're just sitting there, and maybe it doesn't look like anyone's inside.

You drive by, maybe you think *God, I'm glad that's not me,* and you go on. You don't stop, probably, and so you don't know if there's really anyone there, in the car, waiting for someone to fix the engine or fix a flat.

Most of them are for real, and two seconds after you pass, some poor guy's cursing you and yours for not stopping, lending him a hand.

Some aren't.

They're the ones not near any real light.

They're the ones where you can't hardly tell the color, and the windows look black, and it doesn't look like there's any trouble, but you can never tell, it could be a blown hose, something like that. Sometimes the hood's up, sometimes you catch a glimpse of a jack and tire iron near the back, sometimes there's a kid sitting in the grass.

It's quick.

In and out of your headlights so fast, you're not even sure you saw what you saw.

But if you had stopped, five minutes later the place would be empty, no cars, no people.

You'd be dead, Rachel.

They'd say: Just one more stupid woman, out alone when she shouldn't be.

That's dangerous, though, the lures like that. Sometimes people fight back, sometimes they're a little stronger than they look.

The lures are mostly winter rules, when people stay inside.

Most of the time they cruise the back roads, the small towns, the hollers when they're down here in the South. They mostly keep away from the cities. Too many people.

No; too many strong people.

I'm not sure how to explain it because I'm not really sure myself, but there are times when I think . . . I think they can smell death on you. Not that you're dying, cancer or something, but that you're just not ready to go on living anymore. It all has to do with weakness. Physical weakness. Mental weakness. It doesn't matter if you're old, if you're like me, if you're a kid. Weakness, that's all.

Carrion.

Walking, breathing carrion.

Herds are a society, did you know that? There's good guys and bad guys in zebras and lions and whatever you can think of. Sounds dumb, but it's true.

Herds have their garbagemen, too. I know you know that. Sometimes they work alone, sometimes in pairs, sometimes in packs and flocks. Vultures, buzzards, crows, you name it. Hyenas.

Jackals.

Picking off the dying. Taking care of the dead.

They circle around, staying just out of reach, keeping mostly to the shadows where they can wait, where they can watch.

The herd doesn't care. It can't survive, dragging the weak and the old and dying with it all the time.

Trouble is, jackals, like hyenas, don't always follow the rules.

Trouble is, Rachel, when they're hungry, they gotta eat.

They ride mostly at night.

They hunt mostly at night.

They find . . . they find a kid, not even twenty-five, like Maryanne Scott, her car broken down in some godforsaken place in Kentucky, south of Lexington. She reckons the folks that finally stop, they're going to help her with her car, a junker that shouldn't have even been on the road in the first place. She doesn't know. Nobody knows. She doesn't care, either, because she's had a hell of a battle with her family, and she's going to prove every damn one of them wrong, by God, and then, when she's proven it, when she makes it on her own, she's going to ram it down their throats and laugh while they choke. Especially her pig-headed brother who thinks he knows it all.

The police found her before they were done with her.

She'd been skinned chest to knees.

Lord, parts of her were gone.

One of the cops, an older guy just hanging around 'til he could get his pension, head for Arizona, he met me in a bar after the funeral. We got drunk, I guess, talked about just about everything. You know, it helps being rich, but it helps more looking like I do. You put a tailored suit on me, I look like a clown; stick me in a pair of jeans, I'm one of the guys. I'm not young enough to look stupid, not old enough for folks to think I'm one step away from senility and drooling.

So we talked.

Next night we talked again.

Third night we were practically friends, damn near brothers, and the bar was empty, nothing going on the jukebox, and he says to me, *fella, they ain't never gonna catch the guys that did this.*

He tells me why, and tells me why no one's gonna believe me if I make a stink, make a holler, try to warn the whole damn world what's going on, in the dark.

I figured he was drunk, that's all.

I kept asking around.

I spread money, posted a reward, took a practically permanent room in a motel and generally made myself so unpopular, the local cops were ready to run me in on general principles, just to get me the hell out of their way.

One night the old guy comes to the door. Get the hell up, he says, and come with me.

I did.

He was off-duty, and we drove for over an hour, maybe two, him not answering my questions, and I stopped asking after a while. Eventually we came up this road in the hills, and he slowed down, not much faster than a walk. He says he heard they were around this week, but he wouldn't tell me who.

I thought he was drunk again.

He was shaking like a leaf.

Then we come down into this valley mostly farms and such, and he tells me that when we get back to the motel, he wants ten grand. I got pissed. I thought he was shaking me down, and I almost laughed because he was a little bigger than me, but my hands were free. I couldn't lose.

Ten grand, he says again.

Why?

Because when I show you this shit, I'm heading out West and I ain't coming back.

I didn't know what in hell he was talking about, and I tried to tell him I don't pay that kind of money for extortion, not from a guy like him.

Then I saw something in the field off to the left.

Something running.

Something large.

He saw it too, kind of sucked in his breath, and pulled a gun from under his shirt.

I figured I was a dead man.

He'd stop the car, his buddies would come out of the bushes, and I was a dead man.

But he didn't stop.

And that dog, which is what I figured it was, ran through the high grass, too far away for me to make out much more than a vague shape.

It angled toward the road.

The cop rolled down his window.

Then I saw another one, this one on the right, and two more beyond it.

The cop asks me if I can shoot, I tell him I can, pretty good, and he tells me to get the gun he's got in the glove compartment. I did.

There were five of them now, two on one side, those three on the other.

Large.

They weren't dogs, but they were running on all fours.

Then one of them leaps the fence, hits the middle of the road, and stands up.

The cop stopped, and I thought I'd gotten drunk myself.

It was a man.

He stood in the middle of the road, hands on his hips like he was daring us to do something. Smiling. Standing there, just smiling, and shaking his head.

You ever hear the expression, scared spitless?

It happens.

I was.

When the car rolled up a little, the headlights caught him full in the face.

His eyes glowed white, the white spreading a little over his face.

Not a pretty white or a soft white, not even the kind of white you think about when you think about ghosts.

Moon white.

Dead white.

Then he laughed.

So did the others.

Then the cop turns to me, points a finger and says, jackals, sticks his left hand out the window at the same

time and fires a shot, then jams his foot on the pedal. The
man . . . the jackal . . . I don't think he was hit, or hit
badly, but he got out of the way damn fast.

When we went by him, I turned to look, maybe get off
a shot of my own.

But I didn't.

I couldn't.

He was kneeling on the shoulder, the others standing
back behind the fence.

That red glow from the taillights caught them all.

Their eyes still glowed white.

End of story.

I've been down here ever since.
Like I told you, it's what I do.
I hunt jackals.

H e rocked back on his heels and searched her face for belief, or disgust, or something in between. She said, "Are they . . . ?" She rubbed her cheeks harshly with her palms, pushed her hands back through her hair. "Are they human?"

He reached down and grabbed a stone, tossed it up and caught it, then flung it away over his shoulder with a hard snap of his wrist.

"Well?"

He used the door to help him to his feet. "What does it matter? You saw them."

Her look told him that wasn't an answer.

He looked over at the spot where the Caddy had been, where the bodies had been. Empty, now, except for Maurice walking toward him.

"I'm not sure," he said. "But yes. I think they are."

T he living room was warm, one lamp glowing.
Rachel was in her room, James in the shower, and Maurice stood at the window, hands clasped behind him, watching Nola leave her car, a cardigan caped over her shoulders, her waitress uniform still on.

His jacket was off, tossed onto one of the chairs, and as she headed short-stride for the porch, his thumbs hooked around the tartan suspenders he used not to hold his pants up but to give his fingers something to do besides trace webs in the air. He stared through his reflection, but he saw it anyway; he didn't like it. It was a ghost.

Nola's hurried footsteps on the redwood flooring only made his jaw twitch; he didn't turn. He believed, when times were calm and all he had was his church and his children to lead through the times that made them cry, that what he did with James wasn't wrong. Even scavengers were prey. But each time it happened, the fire and the smoke and blood painted on the ground, he doubted; each time it happened, he returned to his house and went down to the cellar. There was a room there, made by his own hand, with no windows and no light. He would sit there on a stool, the door closed and locked. His angels locked him in. They would not release him, not even if he screamed.

When he screamed.

Which he did when the jackals came through the walls and stood before him, watching, weeping, begging him

with their eyes to understand how it was and how it had
to be, demanding he pay penance, showing him the Hell
he had carved for himself.

Every time.

And every time he screamed, but only when the children spat at him and cursed.

"How many?" Nola asked quietly, slightly out of
breath.

He held up four fingers.

"Modeens?"

He nodded.

She dropped onto the couch; he could see her ghost
too, below him in the glass. "Peter called. He told me
about Charlie." She looked around, leaned over and
rubbed one ankle. "He's in the bathroom?"

He nodded.

"Why didn't he tell me at the restaurant? He was there.
Why didn't he tell me?"

"I don't know."

"You wouldn't." She shook her head. "What about
the girl?"

Maurice turned, turned the leather chair and took his
time sitting, every bone resisting, every muscle demanding he stand until he dropped. There would be no cellar
room tonight; penance would come some other way.

"Bedroom," he said, crossing his legs. "The child
never said a word all the way back."

"Well, hell, Maurice, do you blame her?" She looked
around again, then went over to the sideboard, opened a
door, and pulled out a bottle. "Ice?" She made a sound
that resembled a laugh in name only. "Never mind. You
wouldn't pollute it."

He didn't answer.

She filled three tumblers with bourbon, handed one to him, put the second by the table next to the other chair, and took hers to the couch. Sat. Drank. Leaned her head back and stared at the ceiling.

"Goddamn Charlie."

He brought his glass to his lips, smelled the liquor and felt his stomach turn over. But he sipped, sighed, and sipped again. It tasted too good; he didn't deserve it. He put the glass down and watched as the waitress toed off her shoes and curled one leg to the cushion, pushing herself into the corner, tucking her ankle beneath her rump. Her white blouse was open three buttons down, her skirt rode high above her knees, stockings shimmering in the light. The dim glow made her look ten years younger than she was.

She winked at him over the top of her glass. "You like?"

He stiffened. "Babylon is what you are."

She shook her head angrily. "Don't start, Maurice, okay? Lay your guilt somewhere else. Don't start with me."

"Problems?"

His hand shook when he saw James in the doorway, toweling off his hair, no shirt, his feet bare.

"Hey," Nola said, patting the cushion beside her.

James ignored her and walked to his chair, picked up his glass, and stood beside the window.

Maurice prayed that just once the man would show some remorse. "We killed four people tonight, James. That's problem enough."

James shook his head. "No, we didn't. We killed jackals, remember?"

"They're people."

Nola grunted derisively.

"What do you know?" Maurice demanded, pointing a long finger at her. "What can you possibly know?"

"Oh, give it up," she said wearily.

He stood. "I'm going outside for a while." He stared at her pointedly. "To pray."

She said nothing, only looked away.

"Babylon," he muttered.

"And you were a pimp in New Orleans before you got saved. Big fucking deal."

He didn't respond. It was no use. She wouldn't listen. She didn't know.

And as long as James believed too that these creatures weren't human, he wouldn't know either what they had done.

Shade pulled, curtains drawn, Rachel sat crosslegged on the bed, hugging herself, rocking.

She didn't make a sound.

Jim lifted his chin. "You trying to seduce me?"

"Aw, Jesus," Nola said, grabbing her shin, rubbing it. "Not you, too. It's hot, okay? and I didn't have time to change after Peter called me." She rolled her eyes and drank. "Lord."

"It was a joke, Nola."

"Sure. But I ain't laughing."

They seldom did after a night like tonight. It didn't matter how righteous they felt when they started out, all of them or just a couple, and it didn't matter how many of the others there were, one or a handful—when it was done and the site cleared if it had to be, no one felt like laughing at all.

He didn't really understand it. There ought to be relief that the tension was over; there ought to be a sense of mission accomplished, something like that; at the very least, there ought to be gratitude that the number of scavengers had been cut down once again, which meant one less prey would be slaughtered.

But there never was.

Not even with Charlie.

And when Maurice got into one of his damn moods, it was almost enough to make them want to slit their wrists.

"You know what rubs me about this?" he said, speaking to the moon.

She didn't answer.

"Ruby."

Nola sat up. "That bitch? She was there?"

He nodded.

"Oh, shit, Jimmy."

He paced to the wall, stretched his neck, turned and paced back. "Charlie said they were down in Birmingham, the Modeens. Pretty much the lot of them, he figured. It's possible Ruby just wanted to have a little fun."

"She hated your guts."

"I don't think she planned on getting caught, Nola.

She might have wanted to draw me down there." He dropped into the chair, propped his bare feet on the coffee table. "Or maybe she just wanted to tell me I couldn't touch her, not with the rest of the pack just a few hours away."

Nola put her glass down and started to work on her hair, unbraiding it as Maurice returned, Peter Ryman behind him. The younger man went straight to the sideboard to pour himself a drink. When he had, he turned around, leaned against it and sighed. Loudly. Jim didn't ask if all went well. He never did; it always had.

"So now what?" Peter said.

"Well, I want to know why the Modeens are here," Nola said, using her fingers to brush her hair straight.

Jim watched Maurice's face as he said, "Charlie told me there was more. He didn't get a chance to finish, but I think he meant more than the Modeens."

The preacher closed his eyes slowly, drew his lips away from his teeth as he hissed his breath in.

Nola drew her other leg up, huddling now. "Damn, so soon?"

"Been ten, eleven years," Jim reminded her.

"Not long enough," she muttered.

He knew what she meant. So did Maurice, who pulled a handkerchief from his hip pocket and mopped his face and head; he was sweating badly, his skin gleaming in the faint lamplight. Jim wanted to reach across, touch his arm, but it wouldn't do any good.

"What?" Peter asked.

Jim cupped a hand over his chin, pulled it hard down over his throat. "If Charlie was right, the packs may be gathering."

The younger man blinked his confusion, staring into

his glass, lips moving soundlessly, trying to work it out himself.

Jim smiled to himself. The boy, who wasn't really a boy, had a bad case of the stubborns when it came to things he didn't know and felt he ought to. He'd sooner run head first into a brick wall than take anyone's word that the wall was ten feet thick. He didn't like looking stupid, even if he ended up looking more stupid than before.

"If they're gathering," Jim said, hoping he sounded as if he were thinking aloud, "that means the old bitch's dead. Must be getting old, I can't remember her name." He grunted a sour laugh. "I had a feeling Ruby wanted to take her place."

"No feeling about it," Nola told him sourly. "You could see it. If she'd been a little stronger, she'd've done it herself."

He agreed. Ruby Modeen had ruled her family as if she were practicing to ascend a throne. She could be sweet-talking, foul-mouthed, cold, hot, whatever it took. They listened. All the Modeens listened. And since they were the largest pack in the South, it was pretty much taken for granted that what Ruby said was Law, no matter who was nominally in charge of the greater Pack.

He had no idea, not really, how many pack families there were across the continent, how many greater Packs; although they all kept pretty much to themselves, mark-ing their territories, keeping out of each other's hair most of the time, when they gathered, it was as though they were long-lost kin, hatchets buried, feuds shunted aside.

But when the Princess died, they were like a boat without an oar.

Ruby wanted it.

She wasn't going to get it.

"Jim?"

He looked over at Peter, who was still frowning and used his glass to point. "They're gonna be mad, ain't they, Jim? I mean, with Ruby dead and all, they're gonna know, and they're gonna be pissed." He looked at his hand; it was shaking badly enough to slop liquor over the lip. "Oh shit." He put the drink down and backed away from it a step. "Oh damn, Jim, oh damn."

Jim didn't move.

Without looking, Maurice reached around his chair and batted at the air until he caught Peter's arm and tugged at him gently to bring him to his side. Another tug, and Peter reluctantly sank to his knees, sat back on his heels.

"Jonelle's home," he said. "She wanted to come, I made her stay." His eyes closed. Opened. "Oh, man, Jim, this is bad."

Maurice cupped his hand around the back of the young man's head, patted it once, sternly, and patted it again before letting the hand fall away. "You remember that time, spring or two ago, you and me went to Knoxville, that heathen bar near the airport, all that neon inside? You remember that boy with the long neck, carrot-top?"

Peter took a moment before nodding.

"As I recall, that boy had about fifty, sixty friends, right?"

"Well, I wouldn't say—"

"They was all kind of mad, I recall further, because you took a shine to that boy's little lady. Black hair, right? Fancy boots? T-shirt cut off to show her tummy?"

Suddenly Peter grinned. "Yeah. Damn, how'd you—"

Maurice leaned his head back. "Seems to me I recall

that lady wasn't entirely desirous of your affections, either. The boy surely wasn't, no indeed. I remember I prayed hard for your soul that night, young Peter, but you went and took on the whole place yourself."

"He hit me first."

"After you stole a kiss from the lady."

"Broke my damn arm."

Maurice laughed, delighted. "Broke your arm, couple of beauts around the eyes, smacked your left knee good, as I recall. It took my angels three days to put you back together, three days more to get you out of my house."

"Well, hell, Maurice, you had a bottle in each hand and damn near killed half of them."

Maurice kept smiling. "Right."

Peter grinned again, looking at the others. "Some bastard dumped beer on his new suit. I think that's about the time he stopped praying."

Jim winked at him; Nola gave him her *stupid men* look, softened with a brief smile.

He nodded quickly, brushed a hand over his nape. "But there weren't fifty or sixty of them, Maurice."

"Don't matter," the preacher said.

"And Charlie—"

"Was alone," Jim reminded him. "He was alone. We're not."

There was no response, just the sound of his jeans and boots creaking as he rocked forward, rocked back, keeping his gaze from the window.

From the last of the moon.

Then he stood abruptly, dusting his palms nervously against his legs. "Well, guess I'd better get on back. Jonelle'll be having fits. She'll think . . . she'll be having fits, you know how she is."

The others stood as well, and Jim trailed them onto the porch, hands in his pockets, shivering slightly against the touch of the night. Maurice accepted a ride from Peter and left without speaking. Nola slid her arm around his waist and nuzzled his shoulder. "You going to be all right?"

He didn't look at her, but he smiled. "Fine. Just fine."

"What're you going to do about—" She jerked her head toward the door.

"Send her home, I guess. This sure isn't any place for her now."

She slapped his spine and moved away. "You can't. You know that. They know she's here. They know she knows."

"They're dead, Nola. Ruby and hers are dead."

She held up one hand. "Four, Jimmy. There were four in that car."

"So?"

"Ruby had four sons, two daughters, aside from Willum."

He didn't answer.

"Where are they?"

He didn't answer.

"You can't send her back. Gathering or not, you put her on a plane, she'll be dead before she gets home."

She left then, spitting dust and dirt as she backed onto the road, leaving a trail of black tire smoke as she sped toward Potar Junction.

Not a touch, a kiss, a word of goodbye.

He waited until there was nothing left but the dark, a few stars, what was left of the moon; he turned, sighing loudly at his shortsightedness, his stupidity.

She stood in the doorway.

She had something in her hand.

There was something about her eyes.

Nola drove angrily, recklessly, swearing at the night that wouldn't leave her alone. Bad enough Charlie was dead, the idiot hanging around like that when he should have moved on, but she had seen, or thought she had seen, the stir in Jimmy's face when Peter told him he'd left his sister home. She'd seen that look before. It hadn't been for her.

Damn fool.

"Damn fool," she spat, coming out of the tree-tunnel and sneering at Lion's mansion.

If he wasn't careful, that kid would get him killed.

She strangled the steering wheel, snapped at herself for feeling sorry for herself, and wished to hell someone had thought to call her when the hunt went on tonight. The problem was, and she knew it, she wasn't really one of them. A friend. A good lay now and then. Common sense when they needed it. But she'd never been on a hunt, never wanted to go on one, but just once, Jesus Christ, just once she wished they would at least think to ask.

She jammed into the parking lot, kicking gravel to the road, swung around the building and parked at the rear. The heat that stiffened her cheeks and brow settled in her chest after a few minutes' slow breathing.

And finally, a smile.

"What the hell," she whispered as she slid out of her

seat and headed for the back entrance. It was, all in all, better than growing old alone.

She pushed through the deserted kitchen and into the bar. Cider Dunn, paunch emphasized by a T-shirt much too small, arms bulging even when he didn't flex, looked up from his broom. The place was empty.

"You okay?"

"Hell, no, I'm not okay. Good friend of mine got himself killed tonight."

Dunn rested the broom against a table. "Sorry."

She waved the sympathy off. "It's okay."

He headed for the front door, began switching off the lights. "You . . ."

She smiled as he pulled an earlobe, stroked his chin, patted at the few strands left of what he used to call his better'n Elvis hair. He was a cheap bastard, no question about it, and the fact that he looked fat was a plus when a drunk decided he was stronger than God. None of the Junction boys fooled with him. Too many busted heads.

There was only the neon Miller sign left.

"You want company?" he asked from the safety of the dark.

"Sure," she answered. "What the hell. Sure."

J onelle sat crosslegged on her bed, the bed and the room all ruffles and flowers. In her left hand she held a whetting stone, in her right a long-blade knife. The only light drifted in from the open doorway, the only sound

Peter banging around in the kitchen, drinking beer and getting drunk and muttering to himself.

She drew the blade across the stone.

"Jonelle!" he shouted. "Jonelle, I'm hungry!"

She didn't answer.

"Hungry."

She drew the blade across the stone.

She listened to him stumble out of the kitchen and up the stairs, not moving her head until he stood in the doorway, swaying a little, hands at his sides as if ready to draw a six-gun.

"I'm hungry," he said sullenly.

A flutter of dark hair fell over her face as she turned her head slowly. "Go to bed."

"Hungry."

"Go to bed."

He took a step forward, and she looked away, catching ghosts of him at the edge of her vision as he tried to decide what to do next. Finally he muttered, "Hell with it," and lurched away, bounced off the wall and cursed, tripped over something and cursed louder as he staggered into his own room.

She heard him say, "They're gonna know, the bastards, they're gonna know."

A harsh creak then as he fell onto his bed, followed almost instantly by irregular soft snoring.

Then she looked down at her hands and drew the blade across the stone.

Maurice's angels hadn't left.

He prayed in his chapel for nearly two hours, then stripped as he made his way upstairs.

His bedroom was vast, the four-poster immense, and as he fell onto his back, he whispered, "Heaven, children, take me to heaven."

Jim lifted a hand and beckoned her to the porch.

She didn't move until he beckoned again, then padded barefoot over the threshold and propped herself into the corner by the steps, arms folded over her stomach as if she were chilly.

She still had his revolver; after tonight, he didn't blame her.

"Heard a lot?"

A shoulder rose and fell. "Some."

"What Nola said?"

She nodded, staring blindly at the house.

"What do you think?"

Several seconds passed before she looked straight at him and said, "I think Momma's pissed you killed her tonight."

A soft breeze drifted down from the hills, stiffening quickly, hissing across the field, hissing through the trees. Dust lifted from the blacktop, scattered, and lifted again. A twig in the gutter rattled until it popped loose and twisted away into the dark; the screen door slammed shut; a piece of paper in the hallway was chased to the back.

Rachel watched him with faint amusement, his white hair pushed hard over his eyes, his right hand trying to push it away, giving up and reaching out to grip the railing lightly. The porch light shimmered.

He wanted to ask her *what the hell are you talking about?*

He wanted to pass it off as a bad joke, ill-timed and tasteless.

He didn't know whether he should try to kill her or not.

It gratified her, the conflict and confusion, and saddened her a little. This was the bogeyman. This was the nightmare. This is what Momma had warned her against. It had never occurred to her he could be anything more.

A soft sound in his throat, words trying to get out.

She faced him, half smiling, wind squinting her eyes, tousling her hair.

"You knew her pretty well," she told him.

He only watched her.

"She was worse than you thought, though. A lot worse."

When he shifted, she only glanced at the gun. "I'm not

an expert, Jim, not as good as you, but I couldn't miss from here."

He relaxed, just a little, and she watched him furiously, angrily, trying to work it out, where the mistake had come, why he hadn't known her brothers back there at Cider Dunn's.

She felt no inclination to help him.

She felt nothing at all.

The wind blew.

The stars vanished one by one.

"You know," she said at last, wriggling deeper into the corner, shifting her weight, "there are Hunters just about all over the country. You know that?"

He swallowed, but not from nervousness.

"It seems that sooner or later, someone wakes up and figures it out. For one reason or another, instead of dis- believing, they decide to get on their white horse and do something about it." The half smile again. "Nature's way of keeping balance, wouldn't you say?"

He breathed deeply, slowly.

"Momma used to tell us, before you came along there was this old man down near Macon, had an RV fitted out like a tank and stayed on the road all the time. Every day." She shook her head. "Momma said he wasn't much more than a pain in the ass. Bothersome. A fly, you know what I mean? He bit sometimes, but nothing she couldn't handle." A long look, narrow-eyed. "And she did handle it, Jim. When she got weary of him, she did handle it."

He shifted his gaze to the dark of the road.

The wind turned damp.

All the stars were gone.

"She couldn't handle you."

He looked back; no expression.

It didn't bother her.

"You wait. You bide your time. Momma hated that the most. She hated people who had as much as she did. You sure weren't any fly to Momma, Jim Scott."

Nothing; not a flicker.

She knew what he was, knew what he could do, and knew that for the moment he couldn't do a damn thing. Later. Later she'd find out if she had been just as wrong as he'd been; right now she realized she needed him out of her sight. She needed time to consider a hundred questions, one of which was the best way to exploit his weakness. Before, in the planning, in the scheming, she hadn't been sure it would really go this far, and she'd been scared to death; not of the Hunter, but of what Momma would do. When it happened, when he took her in, when she watched and listened, she had almost given up.

Then he had told her about the jackals, and she'd nearly wept in rage at how right he was; and she'd nearly laughed in relief, right there in his face.

She cleared her throat. "Where's Momma now?"

Flatly: "That's Peter's job. Buried somewhere. I don't much care where."

Head and gun shifted at the same time: "Inside."

He obeyed without question, and didn't question her taking him straight to the spare bedroom, didn't argue when she ordered him to strip and lie down on his stomach. The sight of him didn't move her. When she touched him, felt his skin, felt his flesh, as she used the clothesline found in a bottom cupboard to tie hands and ankles to the bed's corners, she felt nothing.

Almost nothing.

A faint shiver, nothing more.

Brushing a hand over a corpse.

Or testing.

She almost laughed aloud then, and wanted to say, *aren't you glad you bought me dinner?* But she didn't. She doubted he'd think it funny, and she had a feeling the irony would only enrage him. Instead, she hummed tunelessly to herself as she worked, once in a while clicking her teeth together, a habit she had never been able to break while concentrating.

And when it was done, the wind slamming against the house and shimmering the panes, she cleared everything off the dresser, the table, and brought it all into the living room and dumped it in the farthest corner. The chair she dragged into the kitchen, from which she took all the cutlery and added that to the pile.

All the while, he didn't move.

All the while, he didn't speak.

She searched his room and found no weapons, closed the door and jammed the lock with a nail she found in the kitchen's utility drawer. He might be able to get in, assuming he could free himself, but not without making a hell of a lot of noise.

Not that that mattered.

She was a very light sleeper.

If he sneezed in his sleep, she would know it and be on her feet before he could step into the hall.

She locked all the doors, checked the windows and locked them. Moving through the small house in her bare feet. Pausing at the bedroom door to watch him at each pass.

Not making a sound.

And when she heard the rain lash the sideboards, she tucked the gun into her waistband and returned to the porch.

Lord, it was good, the rain cool and warm on her face, and she paced for a while, letting it drench her, refresh her, before she made a small sound deep in her throat and vaulted over the railing.

And began to run.

She had no destination, and she wasn't worried about the others—either the Hunter's people or her own—but there was stored, cramped energy to be rid of or she'd be awake all night, and that would be a disaster. She needed to be alert, to be able to outthink him, to be able to hold the reins on her temper so she wouldn't slip, and kill him.

She dropped to all fours.

She ran faster.

A single stroke of lightning over the mountains turned her silver, then returned her to black as she swerved around a tree and raced across a pasture, around the side of a hill, and into a stand of trees trying to dance away from the storm. A small cabin with a light in the back window blocked sight of the road, and she rushed up to it, slammed a fist against the sill, and rushed away, laughing softly.

Tag, she thought, grinning, and sprinted to the blacktop, so glad to be out, so glad to be moving, she hardly felt the effort.

Temptation urged her slyly toward the Junction, to run the streets, laugh aloud, scare every damn one of them half out of their beds and set the dogs to howling.

But she went the other way instead, and another fence, pickets whitewashed and sharp, was easily taken, the mown grass soft and wet beneath her, the sound of her faint in the thunder rumbling through the valleys that split the mountains into teeth. She leapt onto the front porch and stood at the double doors, glancing up at the underside of the porch roof. Then she kicked the doors twice, making them shake, and went from standing to racing as a light flared on overhead.

You're asking for trouble, she told herself when she reached the road again; too clever sometimes means stupid.

She didn't care.

Everything had ached from standing still for so long; now everything felt great.

She slowed but didn't stop, taking the rise and fall of the road at an easy lope, letting the wind do most of the work until she rounded a sharp double bend—what did he call it, the Snake?—and saw the gas station below her. The pump lights were out, bright lights in the food mart to discourage temptation. On a rise behind and facing it was a two-story brick house with a single lamp in a second-story window. Trees looming above it, trying to protect it.

A driveway opened onto the road from the side garage whose back was toward the house, and she walked along the rough blacktop for a few yards, couldn't help it any longer, and ran, circled the house, laughed in explosive delight, and took off, back up the road.

Lightning flared.

This time, when thunder followed, she lifted her head and laughed loudly, as loudly as she could in the lash of the rain.

You were right, Jimmy Jim James, she thought.

Just like a jackal.

Nola sat up, a thin blanket clutched to her bare chest. Cider grunted and rolled onto his side when she poked at him, hissed at him, demanded he get his sorry ass out of bed and go outside, check around. Another try failed to wake him, and she swung her legs over the side and sat there, staring out the window at the trees in back.

Nothing moved.

Only the wind.

A cool wind on a warm night that made her feel cold.

There were too many gaps and gouges in the walls, in the roof; over the rain, under the thunder, she thought she could hear giggling, and laughing, and someone whispering beneath the window. It made her colder, and she hugged herself, slipped back under the blanket and lay on her back.

Watching lightning shadows dart across the ceiling.

When Cider reached for her in his sleep, she grabbed his hand and held on.

Watching lightning shadows dart across the ceiling.

At the crash downstairs, Maurice leapt from his bed and raced into the hallway, not caring that he was naked. His angels moaned sleepily, and he hushed them with a gesture, cocked his head and listened to the last echoes of the knocking settle into the dark corners. Then he hurried down the carpeted staircase, opened the secret closet door, and took out the shotgun he had cleaned and replaced only a few hours ago. From the dining room he carried a chair much too hard for much comfort and set it squarely before the front doors.

He sat, cradled the weapon, and listened to the storm.

When lightning flashed, the stained glass looked too bright, almost obscene; when thunder came, the whole house went black.

He wasn't sure, but he thought he heard laughter, heard someone prowling around outside. But he'd be damned if he'd go out there, just to put his mind at ease.

A holy thing had been done tonight, and now the Devil had come to haunt him.

Jonelle woke when she heard Peter throwing up in the bathroom. Disgusted, she closed her eyes, willing the storm to go away, willing her dreams to start again.

When she heard it out there, heard the laughter above the rain, she threw aside the coverlet and ran to the window, wearing nothing but a T-shirt that barely reached to her waist. From here she could see the back of the station glowing on its tarmac island, the overpass, and the interstate beyond; and the black of Potar Ridge rising on the far side of the long road to town.

There was nothing out there.

Rain sheeted and steamed, the wind tried to get through the pane, but there was nothing out there.

Gooseflesh prickled her buttocks, her thighs; right hand absently rubbed left arm.

Peter groaned.

Then something laughed in the yard, first below her, then away.

She backed away until the bed touched her, ready to call her brother, rolling her eyes when she heard him topple slowly to the floor and begin his snoring again. She reached over to the dresser and picked up knife and whetstone, pushed until she sat in the center of the mattress, and listened as hard as she could, frowning so deeply her brow began to ache.

She heard the horn of an eighteen-wheeler, and the distant crawl of thunder.

And her hand was trembling badly as she drew the blade across the stone.

Ｈe had refused to permit himself a show of heroics. Small satisfaction, but it was enough for a while.

Damaged pride stung, but the anger was worse. Not at being fooled, because there had been no signs, no clues. He wasn't a god; he didn't know it all and couldn't conjure images with a mystic pass over a crystal ball. And not at being humiliated, because he hadn't been, and he wasn't. Go up into the Smokies and track a spoor, sometimes the prey left false signs and sent you down instead of up. It was part of the hunt. Fair enough when one of the parties was going to die.

No.

It was the ease of it.

Construct a reliable fortress, develop the plan, set the guards, make the forays, make the kill . . . and nobody notices the damn crack in the wall, just wide enough to let the enemy take a good look inside.

And slip in without so much as a ripple or a sigh.

Every few minutes he stirred to keep from stiffening, and tested the clothesline half-heartedly, knowing it gave him just enough slack to keep his skin from burning, and placed just so to keep him where he was. At one point, he had no idea when, he imagined himself gathering every ounce of strength for a prodigious heave and tug, except that all he did was flip the bed over and smother.

The image almost made him smile.

What kept the smile distant was the sheet drawn up to his waist. He hadn't heard her return, hadn't heard her in the room. That meant he had dozed. All the anger, all the questions, and eventually the boredom of it, of lying face down, naked, tied to his own bed, had put him to sleep. Not exactly the stuff of gallant warriors.

The room was warm, almost stifling. After closing the house down, she had turned the air conditioning off, and he could feel the sweat begin to bead along his spine, at the backs of his knees; it wouldn't be long before the sheet beneath him became clammy.

He shifted as his shoulders began a subtle nagging ache, the springs creaked, and she was there.

The door was behind him, but he knew she was there.

When he raised his head briefly, her shadow was on the wall, not a foot from his brow.

Watching.

"I'm not going anywhere. You don't have to keep checking."

His voice was rough, his throat dry.

He sounded helpless.

But her silence was worse.

"I met him, you know."

She didn't move.

He stared at the wall. "His name was Bert. Bert Maddock. The man in the RV. You wouldn't know that. But did you know he was damn near sixty-five? I should be in such shape at that age. He had flyers. Made them up himself, copied them wherever he could, handed them out at shopping malls and post offices, places like that. You know why he hated you? Because you made him look like a senile old fart with nothing better to do while he hung around, waiting to die."

He coughed, cleared his throat.

"I only saw him the one time, some roadhouse in South Carolina. I was still feeling my way around, if you know what I mean. He gave me a couple of ideas and told me he'd keep in touch. Haven't seen him since, never sent me a card. I figure he's dead. Right?"

Rain on the window.

The wind crying in the hills.

He wondered if this was when he was supposed to lose control, to beg for his life, beg forgiveness, thrash around and make himself a fool.

"Why didn't you do anything?" he asked instead. "You had a gun. You let them die without a fight. Why didn't you do anything?"

She was gone.

His cheek sank a little deeper into the pillow, and he allowed himself a twitch of a knowing smile. She didn't have to answer; unless he had lost it all in a couple of hours, he already had a pretty fair idea:

She wanted Ruby's place.

A woman like Rachel, as far as he was able to understand her, wasn't ever going to be content sitting on the side like a good little girl, letting the others do her thinking and all the work. Maybe Ruby knew it; maybe she didn't.

The shadow returned.

A hand touched his shoulder, and he waited a second before turning his head.

She knelt beside the bed, a glass of water in her hand, clearly disappointed he hadn't jumped or made a sound.

It was awkward, the drinking with her holding the glass, and some of the cool liquid dripped to the pillow; but all the while, his gaze didn't leave her face, those eyes, a gaze as dead as he could make it.

When the glass was empty, she sat back, knees pulled to her chest, fingers locked over her shins. Her hair was wet, her shirt still damp and clinging darkly here and there to the turn of her figure.

are they human?

He watched her.

yes, I think so.

He wasn't sure.

"You should get some sleep," she told him.

"I would if you'd stop sneaking around."

That startled her. "You can hear—" She looked away.

Well, he thought; score one for the dopes.

A gust of wind snapped rain pellets against the pane and rattled the gutter. He could hear the thunder lumbering east toward Virginia.

Her eyes narrowed. "If you think I'm going to respect you, even if—"

"Honey," he said dryly, "why the hell should you? I don't respect you at all."

He almost closed his eyes when she rose angrily and slapped him. More than a slap. It was a resounding punch, and it hurt, and his vision swung for a few seconds, blurred by unwanted automatic tears.

When it cleared, she was gone.

He closed his eyes, sighing a scold at his big mouth, and opened them again, sighing again when he realized he'd fallen into another doze. The sheet was still at his waist, but his left leg had been cut loose, and he had pulled it up in his sleep. A test proved his wrists still securely bound to the bed, and his other leg was in the warning stages of a cramp.

Though he could still hear the rain, the wind had eased.

He supposed he should be thankful she hadn't killed him yet; but he didn't think she would. Had that been her idea, she would have done it long ago. On the porch. Her kind didn't play with their victims. There was the hunt, and the kill, nothing more than that.

Not, he thought sourly, unlike his own, self-appointed role.

He frowned.

On the porch . . .

Damn.

Dope is right.

Of course Ruby knew what Rachel wanted.

He had no idea how much of Rachel's cross-country story was true, but the chase at the end was; he was sure of it now. Over the years he had been here, there had been other pretenders to Ruby's traveling throne, and they all had been dealt with, one way or another. He

knew Maurice believed the incident a trap, Rachel showing up when and where she did. What that didn't explain
was the how—the injuries, the battered car.

He thought he had it now.

Rachel was a threat, a major one, so she had to be
killed.

He was a threat, a constant one, and he had to be killed;
they were tired of waiting.

Two birds, one Caddy.

Cat and mouse, hide-and-seek.

The rain stopped.

The wind returned, herding the clouds, clearing the
stars, exposing the dying moon.

He wished he could roll over on his back.

He wished he knew what the hell Rachel wanted now.

He wished to hell and God Charlie Acres was here.

She sat in his chair, legs tucked beneath her, staring at the
dark.

The gun was on the table.

T he rust-pocked car paid no attention to speed limits and curves. It hissed through the storm's remnants, mist billowing in its wake.

From the back seat: "I keep telling you, you don't listen, and this ain't right. We should've called the others. They're not that far away."

The driver shook his head emphatically. "No call."

"You're wrong. We ain't dealing with road kill, you know. This is Scott we're talking about here."

"Still and all."

"This is stupid."

The woman in the passenger seat twisted around, folded her arms across the back and rested her chin. "You calling me stupid, Wade honey?"

Wade Modeen, barely out of his teens, naturally lank and naturally pale, gave her a disgusted look. "What I'm saying is, there's three of us and five or six of them." He rolled his eyes in exasperation and stared glumly out the side window. "He's a Hunter, Ruthann. You keep forgetting, that son of a bitch is a Hunter."

Ruthann smiled, tilted her head. "No. He's human, honey. And the human's going to die."

A snarling in his throat, soft and angry and filled with frustration. He leaned forward suddenly, forcing the young woman back.

"Momma is dead, you stupid bitch! Willum, all the others! Ain't you been paying attention here? And who the hell knows what's happened to Rachel, what she's up to?" He held the glare, then slumped back, exhausted. "You don't know, Ruthann. You don't know."

She said nothing for a moment.

The car sped on.

With her back to the windshield, she glanced at the driver. "What do you think, Bobby?"

The driver raised one hand: *don't get me involved.*

She curled her lip at him, and rested her spine against the dashboard.

"Momma couldn't kill him," Wade reminded her sullenly.

"She didn't want to."

A raccoon wandered onto the shoulder.

Bobby Modeen ran it over.

Ruthann turned around. "She didn't want to," she repeated softly. "She could have. She just didn't."

Wade lifted a helpless fist. "Ruthann—"

She stopped him without saying a word, just a subtle shift in her posture.

"Wade honey, don't whine. You keep whining like that, Ruthann's gonna think her little brother is scared."

Bobby reached out and touched her leg, a caution.

She looked.

He shook his head. Slowly. Just once.

Her mouth opened to protest and scold, but his hand squeezed tighter.

"This is stupid," Wade muttered.

Bobby nodded. "You're right. But Momma's dead."

Jonelle overslept.

When she realized the time, she swore at the ceiling and rushed to get dressed. It was well after 10, and Peter would already be down at the station. Not that there was a real ton of work to do. Ever since he had closed the garage bays down, there wasn't anything but the food mart, an occasional tow, and doing private, after-hours work on trucks and cars brought to him by friends and friends of friends. Nothing on the books. Cash in the pocket.

She handled the counter and the paperwork, gossiped with the tourists and truckers, and watched the wheels go by on Interstate 81. She had to admit the site was a lucky one—folks coming down out of Virginia had a chance to fill up before the long stretch to Knoxville, and for those heading the opposite way, Peter kept the prices a bit lower than Bristol. She had also worked a deal with the night manager over at the Ramada Inn in Morristown— late-night travelers looking for a place to snooze before they slammed into a ditch only had to ask, after a little coaxing. She made the recommendation, and took a few bucks back in return.

Nothing on the books.

Cash in the pocket.

After a quick shower, she yanked on T-shirt, boots, and jeans, grabbed breakfast in the kitchen, and stood at the back door while she ate, watching the trees brush off the last of the night's wind. The sky was clear. The air mint beneath the cedar and pine grove. The yard needed mowing but wasn't awful yet, and a trio of crows strutted single-file through the grass left to right, looking for all the world like they were heading for the garage, ready for an outing. She smiled at the fancy, and, thinking about the garage, wondered if Peter would have time for a change to take a look at her bike. It hadn't been firing right these past two weeks, but despite her daily nagging, he kept putting her off.

He didn't like her owning it, didn't like her riding it, and told her the reason the guys she liked didn't like her was because sooner or later they got the idea she was some kind of biker chick. Tennessee was the wrong state, honey, for a reputation like that.

But mainly it was because the work would get him all greasy and sweaty, and he always, but always, wanted to look right for the ladies.

She loved her brother dearly, pain in the butt that he was, but sometimes she had to wonder just where in hell he came from because he sometimes sure didn't act like real kin.

An apologetic look at her garden, vegetables and flowers straining for care, and she decided to make some calls. Peter could wait on the market customers himself. After last night, he deserved it, all that fool drinking, leaving it all in the john. Idiot.

The first call was to UT in Knoxville, her alma mater, source of once in a while once-a-week night classes to keep her hand in and her brain from turning to mush. A moment later she scowled and hung up. The prof wasn't in, and she'd been hoping to get some hours in during registration, helping him with course guidelines, student lists, donkey work that only minimally involved dancing away from his hands.

Nothing on the books.

Cash in the pocket.

More than once she had considered asking Jim for a loan. Nothing much. Just enough to get her relocated anywhere but here. Her brother was her brother, after all, but Potar Junction and the interstate were not her idea of making best use of a liberal arts education. Too bad she hated kids; she could have at least been a teacher.

She hesitated before dialing again, a forefinger drifting into her hair and twisting strands, tugging, twisting them again. A glance over her shoulder as if she'd find him there, waiting on the back stoop, or a massive thunderhead blotting out the sunlight. No such luck.

She dialed anyway.

That woman answered.

"Jim there? This is Jonelle."

"Sorry. He's in the shower. You want me to tell him something?"

Jonelle glared at the wallpaper, disgusted at herself for the reaction. "No, no problem."

"You want him to call you back?"

"I—no, that's all right." She turned, put her back against the wall, the coiled phone cord twisting around one finger. "Thought you'd be gone. Home, I mean. Rachel, right?"

The woman laughed pleasantly. "Yes. And so did I, but he said he had something to do today, I think it has something to do with his friend. Charlie? So I guess I won't be out of here until late this afternoon."

"Oh. Well, look, you want some company, a free

lunch, give me a holler. Call down to the station, I'll be out like a shot." She lowered her voice, sharing a secret. "You have no idea how boring it is there."

"You know, I just might take you up on that. We really didn't get to meet last . . ." The words faded.

Jonelle nodded. "Just give me a call. And tell Jim, he'd better call, too, I'll have him strung up."

She reached over her shoulder to replace the receiver, not moving her gaze from a portly blackbird she spotted, grazing the back yard. It shifted as she watched, shimmered, grew larger, became a dog, then a huge dog that turned on her and bared its fangs.

Dripping blood.

She started, and the illusion vanished.

When the phone rang over her head, she yelped and stumbled away, holding one hand to her throat until she knew her heart wasn't about to leave her. Chiding her skittishness, she took the call and told Peter, no, she wasn't lounging about in the tub or painting her damn toenails, she'd be down in a few minutes, suffer, you dipshit, hungover bastard.

Then she ran up to her bedroom, slipped the knife into a molded leather sheath she'd made herself four summers ago, and clipped the sheath onto her belt at her right hip. A quick pose before the mirror, a few practice snarls and glowers and as many menacing squints as she could manage; a three-note laugh at the ludicrous reflection that didn't so much as grimace back; another knife she slipped into a sheath she had sewn to the inside of her left boot.

Four years ago and a day, such a gimmick would have been unthinkable, a stunt for the movies.

Four years ago and a day, she had picked Peter up in Tampa, and had a flat on the way home, at the edge of a swamp. Her brother had just finished replacing the tire when a pickup pulled onto the shoulder behind them, high beams on, a man opening the door as he wanted to know if they needed a little help. Peter had said, "No," and the man had said, "Too bad."

That was the first time she'd heard the laughter.

There had been two, but Peter had the tire iron and temporarily cut the number to one before she'd gotten out of the car, glove-compartment pistol in her hand.

The second one was fast. Ghost fast in the swamp mist, and Peter was down, moaning, and a hand was around her throat, lifting her off the ground, the gun twisted from her hand.

"Pretty," the man said, turned easily and showed her to his partner climbing up from the shoulder.

That was the first time she had seen the eyes.

And for the first time saw the giant, who stepped out of the dark, heard a curse, heard the fire, and the next thing she knew she was in a huge automobile with Peter stretched unconscious across her lap, a makeshift bandage across his mouth, and the automobile was floating silently north through the dark.

"You would have killed them," the giant had said without turning around.

"Damn right," she answered hoarsely, throat still burning from the man's grip.

The giant nodded, and an hour later said, "There's someone you should meet."

Four years ago.

Now she wanted to tell Jim what she had heard the night before. She wanted to tell him right away. She knew as well as Peter—who had complained about it from the second he had walked in the door—that Ruby had more blood kin, she wasn't sure just how many, and since all those others had been taken care of, the rest might have gotten here much sooner than she feared.

But she didn't know how they had known.

She did know, she was positive, that they hadn't already been around at the time the Modeens had been trapped. Ruby would never have allowed herself to be caught like that, not if there were others and she'd been planning an ambush.

So they hadn't been here already.

But they were here now.

And if that were true, someone must have made a call.

On the other hand . . .

She groaned aloud to shut off the speculation before she made herself dizzy.

"Lord," she muttered as she hurried out the front door, "you do go on, don't you."

Nevertheless, she made a careful circuit of the house, knowing the search for prints was futile, but doing it anyway. Relieved when she found nothing, she pushed through the shoulder-high evergreen shrubs that lined the top of the slope, and slipped-ran down the grass, entering the mart through the back door, closing out the light on a cluttered office just large enough to hold a plywood table she used as a desk, a bulky safe beneath it, and a few shelves packed with Peter's junk.

As she checked the delivery schedule tacked to the wall by the inner door, she heard voices, Peter's and someone else. Since the door was closed, she used the peephole he'd installed two winters ago, then shook her head slowly.

Lord, she thought wearily, you just don't ever stop, do you?

A quick fuss with her hair, and she stepped out into the store. Peter leaned on the counter, making eyes and small talk at a tanned and blue-eyed blonde not, in Jonelle's opinion, worth writing a song over. When the woman saw her, she sputtered, dropped some bills on the counter, and hurried outside. Her car, sleek and shiny, was parked at the farthest of the two self-serve islands, and she didn't look back when she climbed in and drove away. Jonelle grinned. The woman had no doubt come in, all a-flutter, red-cheeked, just smiling up a spring storm, she had no *idea* how to work one of those gas pump things, would Peter mind helping her out, just this once?

Her brother didn't even look around. "Nice work," he grumbled, scooping up the money.

"Just keeping you honest."

He snorted, straightened, and put the bills in the register. "Just keeping the customers happy."

"Ha," she said. "And ha, I'm impressed."

He slammed the drawer shut, fingerdusted the counter. "Sorry about last . . . you know."

She waved a *forget it* hand and walked the aisles, four of them, each shelf jammed with every kind of junk and device any motorist might believe he needed for a long trip, a short jaunt, a ride from here to gone. She checked the refrigerated sections in back, mentally toting the number of beer cases and six-packs, soda, milk, those new fruit drinks every kid seemed to have to have.

For a change, Peter had already put the new newspapers and magazines where they belonged, and had bundled up the old ones for pick-up the next morning.

Guilty, she thought cheerfully; the dope, he's really feeling guilty.

Then he said, "Jo, did you hear anything last night?", and she had no choice but to tell him.

Jim bellowed until she came in, taking her time, although he noticed how she snapped the fingers of her left hand, realized she didn't know she was doing it until he stared and she jammed the hand into her jeans pocket.

"What?"

"I don't care how you do it—hogtie me, hamstring me, put a goddamn pillowcase over my head—but I am *not* going to piss on this bed."

It pleased him when he saw she hadn't thought about mundane things like that, pleased him further when she kicked his jeans to the middle of the floor and said, "When I untie you, put these on."

Then she showed him the gun she had tucked in the small of her back.

"I'm fast," she reminded him flatly. "But you have no idea how quick I really am."

Maurice awoke groaning, every bone in his body protesting, every muscle demanding movement and a dozen magnitudes of atonement. Several fuzzy seconds passed before he realized he was still propped in his chair, facing the front door, his shotgun balanced across the armrests. A blanket had been draped over his lap.

"Oh Lord," he whispered, rubbing sleep from his eyes, massaging his upper arms. "Oh Lord."

His angels were gone. He knew that before he even tried to move. The huge house was empty, and he could no longer hear the echoes of the wind. He blinked at the fierce sunlight unpleasantly distorted through seven stained-glass windows arched over the lintel, turned his head and set the weapon on the floor, his back so stiff he could barely lean over.

"Lord."

He yawned mightily.

He scratched hard across his chest and thighs.

He tried to push himself to his feet, but his legs refused to work, and he braced himself with his arms until the painful tingling eased and he could stand without swaying. The heels of his hands roughly molded the bone and padding of his face as he staggered to the door, took a breath, and opened it.

The color out there slapped at him, the smell of bygone rain wakened him further, and he stood there for nearly a full minute before he realized he was naked.

"Oh, Jesus!"

He slammed the door in near panic and hurried upstairs to shower and dress, refusing himself permission to think of the night before until he was back down in a kitchen large enough to feed the Junction at a single sitting, coffee cup in hand, eggs and sausage on the stove, tinny gospel music on the radio. He hummed as he sat at the white marble table, white wrought-iron legs, and when the meal was at last spread before him, he offered grace and sighed.

It was a bad thing, all that commotion outside. Bad enough he had had to cut down the Devil in four parts, bad enough he still hadn't been able to make James understand that whatever they were, those things were living creatures and not to be slaughtered as if they were cattle raised as fodder, just for slaughter. From the very beginning he had felt there ought to be some ritual, some gesture, some of what he had once told Peter would amount to "preemptive absolution."

It didn't seem right, done the way it was now.

Bad enough, all of it.

But worse was the commotion last night.

Never before had any of them come directly to his home, to the home of his flock.

Never.

This time they had done it twice.

The second time, it had taken some convincing and some loud singing to believe the banging and soft laughter hadn't been a ghost.

He wished it had.

Lord, he wished it had.

But although there were spirits, and a few minor devils making mischief, he didn't believe in any ghost, damned or otherwise.

What he believed in, once he'd calmed down and remembered, were the rest of Ruby Modeen's close kin, drifting out there without their momma, knowing what had happened and looking for revenge. He couldn't remember their names, and wasn't sure now he ever knew them. It didn't matter. They had visited him last night and had told him they weren't going to take this without a fight.

He shrugged.

He scraped a fork over his plate, frowned, and almost smiled when he realized he'd already eaten.

Hadn't tasted a thing.

Hadn't known he'd been chewing.

It didn't bother him that the word had gotten to them so fast. Either they had already been close by and couldn't help but hear all the shooting, or they were . . . he scratched his chin, found the word . . . *linked* somehow. Like identical twins. One knowing instantly when something's wrong with another. It was something he had never had to think about before.

James might know.

He reached out to a tiny white table, picked up the white receiver, and dialed. Still humming.

It was the child, the woman, and he smiled at the high ceiling at the memory of her face.

"It is Maurice Lion, child," he said in his best *don't be afraid* voice. "May I speak to James, please?"

"Oh. Oh, I'm sorry, Mr. . . . Reverend—"

"Maurice," he told her, singing his laugh. "As long as you don't call me what James does once in a while, I think we'll be just fine with Maurice."

"Oh, well, yes. Sure. Thank you . . . Maurice."

"James," he prompted gently.

"He can't right now, Maurice. He's taking a shower. Can I give him a message?"

"Not at all, it isn't urgent. I'll see him later, no doubt, in the normal course of the day." He crossed his legs. "And are you all right this morning, child?"

She hesitated before admitting, "A little shaky, I guess."

"Surely. It's never easy, you see. And for someone like you, it's . . . shocking."

"Yes."

He waited.

She said nothing more.

"Will you ask him to call me, perhaps? I've the Lord's work today, a quick run into Knoxville, but I'll be around most of the time. You tell that boy to remember who's not too big for a whomping."

She laughed and promised.

He laughed in turn and hung up, and spent the next hour cleaning his shotgun and renewing the blessing he gave it before each hunt. The hour after that, in a plain and long white robe, he prostrated himself in the first-floor chapel, praying loudly, practically shouting, until he felt his throat begin to burn. Then he showered, dressed again, and walked into the huge living room just in time to answer the phone. White. On a small white table beside a large white wicker chair.

"Maurice, goddamnit, when the hell are you going to get one of those answering machines. I thought you were dead, for God's sake."

He shook his head as if the waitress could see him. "For God's sake, I am not dead, Nola."

"Jesus, give me a break, okay?"

"If you wish, I'll ask Him." He grinned at her stammering, laughed aloud when she held the mouthpiece away and cursed soundly, as if she were trying to spare him, although she knew damn well he could hear.

"Look," she said at last, "I had a visitor last night."

He nodded. "And me, too, child."

"Did you see them?"

"I didn't look," he admitted. "I had no reason or desire to."

She told him she had figured it was the other Modeens,

since it only made sense they'd want to take care of Jim for what had happened to Ruby. He agreed without reservation, and agreed again when she suggested none of them spend the coming night alone. Bad enough there was a gathering somewhere in the state; they didn't need a minor war raging on their own land.

Something like that, with someone like James, would not go unnoticed, not for long.

By the time they were finished, her anger had settled, calm returned, and a voice he always likened to thick syrup the tempting color of sweet honey. He could listen all night to the words that voice produced, and envied the men who had spent all night listening.

Then: "One more thing."

"Of course, child." Knowing that "child" was the most irritating thing he could call her, and so did it every chance he got.

She ignored him. "It sounds good, you know? saying it was the others messing with us last night. But I can't get something dumb out of my head."

He made a noise; he was listening.

"Only one came around to my place, Maurice. There are four left, I figure, but I only heard one."

"Maybe they were—"

"One," she insisted quietly.

He closed his eyes, and tried to think, to bring back the night, and the sound at his door.

"Well?" she asked.

"I don't know. I think . . . I don't know."

"One," she repeated; a second later she was gone.

"One," he said to the large empty room, and looked through the window just in time to watch the oval shadow of a cloud ripple across the lawn.

She knows it all, Jim thought without any sense of admiration; give it to her, Scott, she pretty much knows it all.

After letting him use the bathroom, the door open wide and her in the hall, and rinse his face with cold water, she made him lie in the tub, head inside, feet on the floor. Then she hobbled his ankles with the clothesline so his stride was no more than half a foot if he pushed it, and brought the rope up to his bound wrists, forcing him to walk in a mild crouch that nearly broke his back.

In the kitchen she made sandwiches, cheese and ham, and gave him two, without a plate. He had to brace his soles on the chair's bottom rung so he could raise his hands high enough to meet his lowered mouth.

The heat had grown worse. All the windows closed, the air still, the sun already glaring in a washed-out sky. He could feel the damning lethargy already starting to slow him down, mind and muscle.

"Who called?" he asked.

"Friends," she answered, hoisting herself onto the counter by the sink. "I told them you were taking a shower."

"Any messages?"

"You're supposed to call them later or they'll skin you alive."

She grinned.

He looked away.

The food tasted like sawdust, the water she gave him tasted laced with iron.

"Sooner or later," he said, "one of them's going to come over."

"Jonelle," she guessed immediately. Shrugged when he stared. "She's got the most time to waste. Maurice says he has the Lord's work to do, and that hooker waitress probably has things to do in that restaurant dump." Another shrug. "I'd bet that boy never does anything his sister tells him not to."

For the first time he felt the heat, across his cheeks and in his chest.

He said nothing; he ate and drank.

"By the way," she said, jumping lightly to the floor. "In case you hadn't noticed, I called my sister last night."

D orry Wardell was still in her teens, with all the awkwardness that implied, a little shyness, and a tendency to repeat every instruction she received so she wouldn't forget it. Nola didn't mind her, because Cider kept her mostly on the register so she'd be restricted to "Have a nice day," and "Was everything okay?" In fact, they got along pretty well, what with Dorry keeping her up on the latest music and dress fads, while Nola worked with her on her makeup and appearance, a fair job considering the girl's naturally pale complexion, bony figure, and child-like voice.

Today, however, her patience had been left behind.

She couldn't get hold of Jimmy, Maurice was as always a goddamn prick, and Cider told her she wouldn't be able to leave early on account of there was this church-outing group stopping by in the middle of the afternoon, and he'd be damned if he was going to leave all the tables to Dorry.

"Sweet kid," he said, his expression making the words a lie. "If she weren't my niece, I'd fire her tomorrow."

"So why the hell don't you get someone else, for God's sake? It's been months since Maureen left."

"I'm working on it, I'm working on it."

'Course you are, she thought; 'course you are. And used the back kitchen exit to get her into the tavern. She sat at the bar, leaned over, and pulled a beer from the small fridge, rolled the can over her forehead, opened it, and drank.

It tasted sour.

She shuddered.

Looked at the mirror behind the bottles and thought she'd better clean that thing some day; and she thought that if Jimmy didn't get back to her soon, there might not be another day around to clean it.

"Oh, nice talk," she told her reflection, and opened another can. "Real nice talk."

She had taken but two sips when she realized where she was.

In a place that, if she screamed, not even Cider in the kitchen would hear her.

"Damn them," she muttered as she slid off the stool. Damn them for taking one of her refuges away.

And just before she left, she said, "And damn you, too, Jimmy Scott."

The one thing Jim feared was Rachel losing her temper; the one thing that concerned him was he losing his. So far, he reckoned he had done a pretty fair job keeping his voice even when he had to speak, his expression blank whenever she looked at him. She appeared puzzled by his lack of reaction—not one escape attempt, not a single moment of pleading, or bargaining, or blustering threats. He doubted she thought him cowed or subdued, but she couldn't quite get a handle on his behavior.

She had him in his chair, angled so he could look out the window, and watch her on the couch without much effort.

He didn't need to.

He had taken every opportunity to observe and judge her since the night before, and had decided to his disgust that he didn't know as much about her and her kind as he had thought. If a stranger walked in now, unaware of anything but what he saw, he'd think no more than she was a very disturbed young woman with a gun.

But the gun was only smoke; he'd have no concept of the real danger he was in.

Jim had known from the beginning that was their strength.

Stop to help someone stranded on the roadside, open the door to someone needing to use the phone or to ask simple directions, and what you see is what you see. Even if you were part of the paranoia of the time, suspecting serial killers and mass murderers in every twitch and jerk of someone whose looks you didn't care for, you couldn't possibly know you'd be better off with Ted Bundy.

But they knew it.

Disbelief was their armor, and their most effective weapon.

He shifted, and tried not to wince at the chafing at his wrists or the strain on his back. If she kept him like this much longer, freedom wouldn't allow him to do much more than fall flat on his face.

are they human?

i think so

He still didn't know.

"Cut me loose," he said at last.

She affected a wide-eyed mild shock, and laid on the accent. "Mr. Scott, whyever would I want to do something foolish like that?"

He turned to the window. More clouds drifted over the horizon, low and dark like newly formed mountains. "You said it yourself—Jonelle or someone might stop by." He looked at her. "You don't want to have to kill them."

She uncoiled from the couch and sashayed over, shaking her head. "And why wouldn't I, Mr. Scott? Jim? Seems to me I have the right. Now." Behind the chair. "After all, y'all killed my Momma, didn't you? Wasn't that part of your marvelous plan to rid the world of . . . what *do* you call them, Jim? Monsters? Don't you want to get rid of all the monsters?"

He ordered patience. "Not quite."

Her weight against the chair, her hand lightly brushing his shoulder. "Jim, you've been thinking too much."

"We killed her for you, Rachel."

The hand froze.

He waited for a blow, a squeeze, the cock of a hammer; what he got instead was a schoolteacher's *good boy* pat on the head, the hand trailing through his hair as she moved back in front of him and leaned close so he could see her eyes.

"So you did," she whispered. "So you did."

Her lips parted slowly, and he couldn't help but see her teeth. White, near actress perfect, brighter by the dark of the lips that framed them, pursed, and drew away again to let him see what he hadn't noticed before—the points. They weren't animal fangs, nothing quite so melo-dramatic as a vampire's fangs, but each tooth he could see ended in a distinct tiny point.

He drew back instinctively.

She drifted around to the side, and he could feel her breath on his cheek, moist and warm.

"Thank you," she whispered.

She kissed him.

He suppressed a shudder.

Another kiss, a little longer.

Feeling the touch of her hair, the soft touch of her lips as they kissed his cheek a third time, and his temple; as her tongue, lightly rasping, traced the outline of his ear.

The teeth.

"Thank you."

He braced himself.

And nails that scratched across his nape as she circled behind him, laughing softly, hardly a sound.

His eyes closed and he refused to breathe until the touch left him, and she dropped into the chair opposite, hands gripping the ends of the armrests, legs crossed. Sunlight through the window was so bright, it might as well have been shadow; all he could truly see were those eyes, and those teeth.

"You came out of nowhere," she began.

All those people, running one place to another, hundreds of thousands of them clumping together like sheep, like deer. The only time they have an idea of what's out there is when they're in bed, just before they fall asleep.

But they forget it by morning.

It's so easy, most of the time.

Most of the time it's so easy.

Then suddenly there you were. Charging out of the herd, knowing just what you were doing, where to look, how to do it.

You scared Momma to death, you know.

You never stopped.

Time would go by, and there'd you be again.

Charging out of the herd.

You just never stopped.

It isn't like there's as many of us as there are of you. There isn't. Not by half. Even if you count us all. Just enough to cull the herd, just enough to survive, Nature's balance, like I said.

But you made us be more careful than we were used to. We had to roam the hills most of the time instead of the highways. Those interstates out there—Lord, you've no idea how easy they made things for us, getting from one place to another with hardly a wink between. Not the cities, of course; maybe once a year, maybe twice, but no more. They're too big, too tempting, too available. They make us lazy.

And when we get lazy, we get caught.

No; we get killed.

Momma was strong, she wanted you dead, but she couldn't get the others to do anything about it. Half of them were too scared, most of the rest didn't want to get you more angry than you were. They sure wouldn't come here. To your territory. That'd be like sticking your hand on a buzz saw, thinking you'd only get a scratch. But Momma kept on, and kept on, and pretty soon she started driving some away, they paid her no mind, and that made her madder.

Made her weaker.

Not weak enough, though.

We had a fight a while ago, a hell of a battle with no one taking sides. I lost, and she decided it was best I ended up dead. Ruthann, my little sister, she's no competition, but I surely was. I spent two months running, Jim. Two months. I never was in California, but I was in Texas, Colorado, down Mississippi until just a week ago. No pack would have me. They knew I wasn't about to turn a new leaf. Much as they didn't care for Momma, won't cry when they hear, they were scared of her too.

So I decided to head up to Virginia, hide a little, lick my wounds, see what came next.

They caught me outside Nashville, just like I told you.

Momma was crazy.

She was afraid of me, and she wanted me so bad, it drove her out of her mind.

That's why she came here.

Jesus, I hated you when you shot Willum down.

I wanted to do it myself.

Maurice was right. It was no accident I came to your door that night. I figured, since I couldn't kill her on my own, you surely would. And I was right. Now you have to do the same to Ruthann.

Mercy, it's hot in here.

Are you hot, Jim?

I sure am.

And you don't have to look at me as if I'm as crazy as she was. Don't ever underestimate me, Mr. Scott. I'm my Momma's daughter, and don't you forget it—I know how to use what's at hand to get what I have to get.

I guess I should have been an actress, after all.

I was pretty damn good, don't you think?

You could look at it this way, if you want to—in less than a week, you'll have gotten rid of seven Modeens. Seven's a lucky number, Jim. Seven gone, then I'm gone.

After that, all you'll have to do is watch out for the night.

W ith his gun in one hand, cocked and at his throat, she cut the line, leaving him to work the knots and wraps himself.

"What if I say no?" he asked, massaging the blood back into his wrists.

"They're coming whether you say no or not."

"You haven't thought this through, you know. To do what you want, I'll need at least one weapon for myself, maybe Maurice or Peter to back me up. What's going to stop me from killing you at the same time?"

She held up the gun.

He didn't blink. "What if I don't care?"

"Before, or after?"

He frowned.

She showed her teeth, just a little. "Before, I'm not worried at all, not a bit. You're not going to pass up a chance to get rid of a Modeen. And certainly not three of them at one time."

"You're awfully damn sure of yourself."

Her voice leveled. "Charging out of the herd, Jim Scott. You can think what you want, but you can't help but charge out of the herd."

"And . . . after?"

She didn't answer.

Heat shimmered up from Potar Road, invisible fire blurring the field beyond.

At the top of the rise, as the white sun took the sky, there was no shade, only less of the glaring light.

The clouds were still there, still spreading slowly out of the west, moving slowly.

He stood, fingers massaging his waist to the small of his back. He was tired of watching the infrequent spurt of traffic along the road, tired of watching a bedraggled one-eyed crow trying to find something to eat in the remains of a squirrel, and he was damn tired of sweating like a pig inside his own damn house. He wondered how long it would be before those damn clouds finally got here.

Aware of her gaze, preternaturally steady, he walked stiffly into the hall and flicked on the air-conditioning switch at the thermostat's base. A glance toward the back door. How quick was she, really? Fast enough to get off a shot before he was through the door? She wouldn't have to concern herself about neighbors—the nearest one north was Maurice, the closest south Jonelle and Peter.

He had wanted isolation.

He cursed it now.

Besides, she wouldn't have to shoot if he got outside in one piece.

It wouldn't take her long to run him down.

In the kitchen he filled a glass with water and drank it without taking a breath, refilled and leaned back against the sink, trying to think, scowling at the stifling heat. A check of the window above the sink showed him nothing. The sun was too bright, trees and grass bleached; no miracles like a wandering horse, a wandering hiker.

Just the heat.

He mopped his forehead with his arm.

He reached into a drawer and pulled out a spoon, tapped it absently on the counter while he waited for the lethargy to pass. It was a way to let her know he was still here, maybe keep her away until he could muster some options.

A hand over his face.

Another glass of water.

The spoon, tapping slowly.

She stood in the doorway, unarmed, head slightly tilted to the right, staring at the spoon, then at him.

Then she was gone.

He heard the hollow silence when the air-conditioning was shut down.

He smiled, raised a quick eyebrow, and placed the glass in the sink. Ran the water, cupped his palms, splashed his face and sighed aloud, following the clear spiral into the drain—as if it might give him a magical answer—before he turned off the faucet and grabbed the hand towel, dried his face, and draped the towel over his shoulder.

Sweat gathered along his spine, under his waistband.

He realized he had begun to breathe through his mouth.

Funny how nobody had bothered to call back, or stopped around to check on him.

Funny how insisting on living alone for so long had formed habits in others, leaving him alone.

His stomach growled; he made himself a sandwich, took a beer from the refrigerator, and ate and drank standing up.

How fast was she? Really.

In the hall he reached for the doorknob, and pulled his hand back. He couldn't think straight. Open the door, bullet in the back; get through the door, those teeth at his throat.

Jesus.

He took his time moving up the hall, not realizing how truly short it was until he reached the living room before he was ready; he leaned against the archway wall, arms folded, and raised the eyebrow again.

Rachel sat on the couch, pushed into the corner nearest him so that all he could see was the back of her head, the curve of the leg pulled up and under. The gun was on the table beside her. It mocked him, dared him, and all he could do was look away in disgust.

He couldn't think.

He reached around the wall and flicked the switch up.

"Turn it off," she said, not looking around.

"I'm dying in here, for God's sake."

"Turn it off." Her voice was slow, throaty, as if she were drowning.

How fast was she now?

He shifted, braced himself, and lunged for the gun.

She turned at the same moment.

He froze when he saw her face—lips drawn back, eyes narrow, a sudden flush smeared across her cheeks.

"Turn it off," was all she said.

He hesitated, not six inches between the reach of his fingers and the gun's handle.

Six inches.

Those teeth.

Those goddamn pale-dark eyes.

He nodded, straightened, and did as he was told, leaned his forehead against the wall and lectured himself quickly and silently on the virtues of prudence and the pitfalls of being stupid. Then he dropped into his chair and let the heat smother him.

It's what she wanted, after all.

She was waiting for the night.

When they stopped for gas, Ruthann put on a pair of oversize sunglasses and stepped out of the car, stretched languidly, and walked around to the trunk, leaned against it and opened her shirt halfway down as she scanned the empty highway, the hills and pastures on the other side. She fanned herself with one hand, squinting, and braced one sandaled foot against the rear fender. Despite the fact she was in the shade of the gas island's corrugated overhang, she might as well have been standing in full sun.

Rachel, she thought, wiping a droplet of sweat from the hollow of her throat, I'm going to kill you personally, I swear to God I will.

Not five seconds later, Peter came out, grinning, pushing back his hair, wiping his palms on his jeans.

"Y'all need some help?" he asked, raising his voice against the sudden blare of a piggy-back truck raising dust toward Knoxville.

He stepped up onto the island and leaned against the pump. She saw him check the car's interior, hard to do with the tinted glass, and puffed up a little to distract him, shifting her leg slightly outward. "Depends," she answered. She looked toward the market. "You alone?"

"Could be."

"You a garage?"

He shook his head, stepping closer but staying up on the island. Looking down.

She obliged.

"Damn thing keeps making noise," she told him.

He slipped a hand into his hip pocket, puffing a little himself. "Your, uh, friends, they don't work cars?"

She grinned. "Not a bit."

He lifted his chin, scratched his neck thoughtfully. "Well, look, I ain't really a garage, no, not anymore. But I've been known to do some work here and there, you know? Friends and all? Emergencies and such? Strictly off the record, of course."

"Of course."

He checked the rear window again. "So. You want me to check 'er out?"

Slowly she turned her head toward the highway. "Damn, it's hot."

"Cooler inside."

She waited a minute before she nodded, took her time looking back. "Bet it is." She pushed away from the car with her heel, patting his stomach with her palm as she passed. "They know how to pump gas." She jerked her head toward the car. "You got cold beer?"

She walked on, knowing he was watching, pausing only when she heard him rap a knuckle against the driver's window, heard the hiss of the pane descending.

"Be better if you turn the engine off," she heard him say, and heard Bobby grunt an answer.

Once inside, she took her sunglasses off, twirling them in one hand. Empty counter to the right, a coffee maker brewing, a row of hot dog spindles, a small display case that held sandwich meats and cheese. She strolled casually across the floor, checking the aisles, seeing no one crouched down there, looking for something on a bottom shelf. A metal door with a peep hole behind the counter, closed.

She turned when she heard the bell ring over the entrance.

"Bitch of a day, ain't it," he said, coming toward her.

She hoisted herself onto the counter, stretched her neck, plucked at the shirt. "Nice and cool in here, though, you were right."

She almost laughed aloud: he couldn't stop his hands, didn't know where to look now that they were alone, didn't know how to pose.

She plucked at her shirt again. "Too cool." Her hand reached out, an inch shy of his arm. "You ever see that John Wayne movie, the one where he's in that old mansion, only a lady left and some servants?" A shift, and her fingers had his sleeve. "She's kind of pretending she don't want anything to do with them, she being a Southern lady and they being Yankee soldiers and all." She tugged, gently. "You know this one?"

He shook his head, ducked it a little, then suddenly checked the window.

"Oh, don't worry about them," she said with a dismissing wave. Another tug, and she had him again, a step closer. "They were at dinner, these soldiers and the lady? She has all kinds of stuff, even though there's a war and all, and she has this big old plate." Close enough now that her knees touch his thighs. "Has lots of chicken on it, you know?"

His expression made her smile, and she very carefully placed the sunglasses on the counter beside her. Her legs parted, and she drew him closer. He was handsome, no question about it, in a young man, old boy way.

Not her type at all.

"Look," he said, trying to be bold, still a little nervous about the car outside.

She ignored him. "So she stands up, see, and she has on this gown, this dress that has a neckline . . ." She used her free hand to trace the image across her chest, as slow as her speech. "Then she kind of leaned over. Like this? Holding the plate of chicken?" She licked her lips and smiled. "You like chicken?"

"I guess."

Her legs wrapped around his, one at a time, carefully, so as not to spook him, and she saw his chest rising, falling, not thinking anymore, she was sure of it. She could smell it as her right hand slid around his neck and up into his hair.

"The lady says," whispering now, close to his ear, "would you gentlemen like a wing . . . or a breast."

He didn't answer, didn't smile, didn't blink.

"What do you want, Peter?"

His hands answered for him.

She sighed, tilted her head as he tilted his, and pushed herself lightly into his palms, and let him kiss her.

Felt him stiffen a moment later, but she didn't let him pull away.

"Hey, how did you know—"

She grabbed his hair, cupped her other palm under his chin, and twisted his head around.

It made hardly any noise at all.

onelle drew blood, biting down hard on the inside of her cheek to stop herself from crying out. The distortion of the peep hole made the view seem unreal, and she had to pull away and blink before she was sure.

Peter was dead.

The woman still had him snared between her legs, one hand holding him away as a large, bearded man came through the entrance, saw them, and grinned. He said something, then turned and beckoned toward the car she had seen at the pump.

They'll check here, she realized with a start, and backed away, hands tight at her sides to keep a spiraling panic from gaining control. A fast scan of the office for something to use against them was futile, too many at once for the knife, and there was no time to open the safe and get the gun Peter kept here. She had to get to the house.

Peter was dead.

She checked the peep hole again. Her brother was gone, the woman still on the counter, stripping the wrapping from a candy bar with her teeth. The bearded man had lit a cigarette, shook a scolding finger at the woman, and bared his teeth in a soft, head-back laugh.

Jonelle nearly doubled over at the sudden nausea that made her shudder.

Oh God, she thought with a stagger-step backward; oh God, they're here.

A clamp fastening abruptly around her head made her dizzy. She reached blindly behind her, found the doorknob, and held on, feeling the anger rise as the nausea subsided, feeding it with the muffled voices she heard in the store.

The muffled laughter.

The doorknob turned.

She gaped at it, holding her breath, trying to remember if it was locked or not.

"Damn," a man's voice said.

"Just break it in," suggested another, sounding a lot younger. "We ain't got all day. Hell, the damn thing looks like plywood."

A wary check outside, and a fearful scan of the slope. It looked so high, a mountain of grass topped by a forest. If she didn't get up there fast enough, if one of them decided to go around the building instead of trying to smash the office door, if the ground was still slippery from the rain, if she fell, . . . too many ifs.

Something struck the inner door.

She ran.

Across the blacktop, using her hands when she reached the slope to pull herself upward, not looking back but waiting for the cry of alarm until she plunged through the shrubs and threw herself to the ground, gasping, not quite sobbing. Her face was drenched, T-shirt clinging to her chest and back, her hair a sodden weight that made her head too heavy to lift. Pushing branches aside, she saw nothing below but the roof of the car at the pump. No movement, no sign of life.

Soon, though.

Soon.

Another sprint even though she was winded, keeping

as low as she could, her back and thighs protesting, eyes stinging and blurring. She didn't dare use the front door, ran around the side instead and fell wheezing, weeping, into the kitchen. Raging. Kicking to her feet and racing into the living room, standing to one side of the curtain-framed picture window, and holding her breath when a man, the tall bearded one, stepped through the office door and squinted up at the house.

Do they know?

He left the door ajar as he returned inside.

It wouldn't be long.

She hurried back to the kitchen and lunged for the wall phone, dialed Jim's number, and cursed, nearly shrieked, when the busy signal sounded. She slammed the receiver back onto its cradle and dropped into a chair, elbows on the table, palms pressed to her temples.

She needed to think, needed a moment however long to settle the whirlwind that used to be her mind.

She couldn't stay.

Peter was dead.

She had to get to the garage, get to her bike, get to Jim's and tell him what happened.

They were here.

A series of slow deep breaths soon calmed her without disarming the rage or dulling its edge.

She tried calling Maurice, but no one answered; she tried Dunn's Place, but the girl who answered told her Nola was too busy and couldn't be reached.

There was no one else.

She was alone.

They were here.

A second trip to the living room; this time the car had been brought around to the back door.

She didn't have to wonder what they had done, what they would do, to her brother. She had not yet seen it firsthand, but she'd heard Jim speak of it often enough so that she leaned heavily against the wall and pressed a fist to her stomach.

They would do it to her, too.

If they caught her, they would do it to her.

A car's impatient horn shifted her attention to the highway, and a ragged line of a dozen vehicles sped west past the station, another line east, this one mostly trucks. Then she thought she saw Maurice's old Lincoln sweep by, but the sun was too bright, and her squinting gave her nothing but the first spark of a headache.

A state patrol car followed a van, hanging back, not passing.

Four bikers in tandem pairs.

An ordinary day in an ordinary hot summer, and they didn't know. None of them knew.

She wondered if the Modeens were going to wait until sunset, hiding out in the market until they had shadows to roam in. If they did, she had a chance to get away without being heard. She could roll the bike across the side lawn, kick it if she had to up the short embankment to the road, and keep going until she was out of sight. The heat would probably kill her, but it was better than doing nothing.

A car pulled in to the pumps then, and she almost found the nerve to throw the door open and scream; but it pulled away after only a few seconds, tires protesting angrily as it swerved onto the service road that would take it back to the highway. Someone had put up the "Closed" sign. Nobody was going to stop; nobody was going to help her.

Leave now!

Oh . . . Peter.

Then they came out of the office, two men and the woman, and one pointed at the house.

W hen will they be here?"

"You worry too much, Jim. Soon enough. You have to be patient."

"What about the others? My—"

"We'll get them when we need them."

"All of them?"

She looked at him, looked at the ceiling, and ran her tongue over her top lip. "I . . . don't think so."

N ola leaned impatiently against the cash-register counter, looking at but not seeing the handful of late lunch customers spread through the booths. Cider yelled something at the cook in back. A fly bounced against the ceiling, over and over. The shrill yell of a small child in the parking lot, the answering shout of its mother.

She had tried Jim twice in the past hour, both times getting nothing but a busy signal. After the second call, Cider had pulled her into the kitchen, red-faced, hands on his wide hips, and reminded her of those church folk who would be here any minute, two buses, who knows how many starving kids and their desperate mothers. Before she could get a word in, he gave her the you're-at-work-damnit-not-home routine she was so familiar with, she could have given it back to him word for word. As it was, her nerves were only drawn more tightly, and it was all she could do from throwing her apron into his face and walking out. It wasn't, she thought as she stared at the diners, as if she really needed this damn job anymore. Her local bank had a nest so deeply feathered she could have traveled first class around the world with two friends and a damn dog, and still have enough left over for a trip back the other way. But she was used to it, it was comfortable, and Jimmy needed her besides.

She rolled her eyes.

Sure, darlin', right.

That man needed her like he needed a hole in the head, and who the hell did she think she was kidding?

The telephone shrilled on the back wall, but before she could step away from the counter Dorry popped out of the kitchen and grabbed it, turning her skinny back on the room. Then a customer called, it was Rye Harden, and Nola went over. He'd been trying for an hour to get her to dinner, using commiseration for Charlie as what she thought was a piss-poor excuse—in your grief, maybe you shouldn't be alone.

Good lord, she wanted to shoot him.

But he was serious, even earnest, and it was hard not to give him a real smile, some honest chatter, all the while glancing over her shoulder.

"You waiting for them magazine people to call?"

She blinked. "What?"

The undertaker grinned, stroking his handlebar mustache. "You know, the one's that give away that million dollars every year?"

"Oh." She tucked the pad into her apron. "Sure, Rye. I live for that moment."

He laughed, and she turned just as Dorry raised a hand to beckon her. But Cider came out of the kitchen, snarled at her, snarled something into the receiver before Nola could get there, and said, "I told you, Nola, this isn't your private secretary here." He patted Dorry's rump to get her back to her station. "You make and take your calls on your own time."

Nola glared helplessly.

Dunn touched her arm, lowered his voice. "Those folks from the church'll be in here any second. Soon's you're done with them, you can take a few minutes."

"Oh, thanks, Master," she said.

He winked broadly, touched her arm again, and left, and just as she reached for the phone, the hell with him, she heard the sputtering exhaust of a pair of past-prime school buses pull into the lot.

"Shitfire," she muttered, and grabbed her order pad again. From the looks of it, the sounds of the unloading, those few minutes weren't going to come for at least a couple of hours.

J onelle watched the two men argue, not very heatedly, one of them still pointing at the house as if he could see her hiding beside the window.

Now or never, she thought, and had taken one step toward the back, when the younger one came back outside, wiping his hands on a towel.

He headed straight for the slope.

Rachel had moved the telephone to the floor beside the couch, and had pulled the plug from the wall.

Jim had argued that his friends would find a busy line suspicious, or alarming, but all she had done was show him her teeth.

"Someone will come," he said for what he thought must have been the hundredth time.

"Let them," she answered lazily.

Maurice was less than twenty minutes from Knoxville center, drifting in the righthand lane down the long interstate slope that led toward the river, when a stone kicked up from a car just ahead and cracked off the windshield. Startled, he yanked the wheel left, heard a truck blare at him, and yanked the wheel in the opposite direction, leaving the lane for the shoulder, where he finally braked to a halt.

His hand trembled on the steering wheel.

The wind of passing traffic punched the old car.

What he had intended to do was make a fast raid on his

supply houses—candles, some new chairs for the chapel, go to the university and talk to that prissy white boy again about the stained-glass windows he wanted as replacements throughout the house, matching the ones over the front entrance. No more than a couple of hours, back in plenty of time for something to eat before he went over to James' house.

Back long before dusk.

While both he and James had had experiences with the jackals in daylight, especially in winter, he knew they preferred to do their traveling and hunting at night. Yesterday had been a fortunate, foolhardy exception; a major exception because Ruby Modeen hated James so much, Maurice was positive she had lost a goodly portion of her mind.

The others, though . . . they may not be as clever, nor as ruthless, but they surely knew better than to try to take their hunter when they weren't at full strength.

At first he'd had the terrifying, exhilarating, idea that the remnants of Ruby's pack would seek help at the gathering, wherever that was, and he had almost rushed right over to James to demand they do something, not wait until nightfall.

The idea passed.

Ruby's kin, no matter what, wouldn't ask for outside help.

The car shuddered in the wake of a long convoy of trucks.

He stared at them blindly, then turned his head until they passed, the glare from their sides too much.

Lord, he thought, if it be Your will, strike those bastards down, they're gonna kill me one day.

Another passed, much slower, and though the reflective back was covered with words, and a cartoon of a grinning possum, all he noticed was a red-and-black rectangle down near the bottom.

For no reason at all, it reminded him of the "Closed" sign Peter used at the gas station.

Then he knew why.

"Oh, Jesus," he whispered, slamming his foot on the accelerator. "Oh, Jesus."

F uck it, Nola thought; I can't take it anymore.

She stomped over to the counter, yanked off her apron, and handed Dorry the order pad.

"What's this for?"

"Something I have to do."

"Jeez, Nola, Mr. Dunn's going to skin you."

Nola stared at her.

Dorry backed away. "What? What'd I say?"

"Tell him I'll be back in fifteen minutes."

"Nola!"

Only one, she thought as she hurried from the restaurant to her car; goddamnit, there was only one.

J onelle slipped the belt knife from its sheath, hefted it, and told herself a dozen times that as long as there was only one, she had a reasonable chance.

He would underestimate her.

One look at her size, and he'd probably grin, maybe laugh, maybe make some kind of wiseass crack once he realized the kind of figure she had.

hey, little girl, your momma know you're out?

They did it all the time.

hey, little girl, you want to see something nice?

Pushover is what he'd think.

Little gal with a little knife. He wouldn't know if she could use it until it was too late to learn she could use it very well.

Better, in fact, than Jim could use his rifle.

She watched as he paced along the base of the slope, obviously trying to decide if there was a short way up to save time and effort. Then he tossed the towel aside and started to climb, knees bent, arms slightly forward for balance. Halfway up, she realized he was younger than she was, his round face red from exertion and looking redder because his so pale, fair hair was flopping over his eyes. Almost good-looking, probably thought he was handsome, probably thought he could get most anyone into his bed.

His gaze never left the house, even when he slipped once and went down on his knees.

She stepped deeper into the room and to one side.

The woman stepped out of the office and yelled.

The man turned and said something, but he didn't stop.

Jonelle decided: he'd come to the door, she'd fling it open and gut him before he had a chance to yell.

The woman called again, and Jonelle realized that she, too, was younger; from the looks of her, barely into her twenties.

The man stopped.

"C'mon," Jonelle urged in a whisper, turning the knife over and over in her hand.

He flapped his hands at his sides and shook his head.

The woman insisted.

"Please," Jonelle whispered harshly, looked down and realized she had been stabbing at the wall. Looked up and saw the man heading back down the slope, hangdog, shrugging, stopping at the bottom and pointing emphatically at the house.

At her.

Christ, Jonelle thought, slipping the knife into its place; Jesus, what the hell are you thinking, girl, you crazy or something? Do him, and that bitch's up here before you can shut the damn door.

Then the woman cocked her head as if listening to someone behind her, and waved her hand, and nodded.

The young man clapped his hands eagerly, blew her a kiss, and took the slope at a run.

Maurice saw the blue light flashing in his rearview mirror.

There wasn't much he could do but pull over, close his eyes, and pray.

Jonelle charged through the house, slammed through the back door and nearly wrenched her arm as she stopped, whirled, and closed the door as softly as she could. She didn't wait to see which way the man would come; she raced across the yard and ducked into the garage through the side door, thankful Peter had as usual forgotten to draw the front door down. His car was here, up on blocks, and her motorcycle, off to the side. She wished she knew if he would search the house first, or come straight through and see the garage; she wished she knew if he could smell she had been in there, waiting for him.

Nervously she tapped the keys in her jeans pocket.

If she started the bike now, the noise would bring him, and she might not be able to reach the road in time; if she waited until he was on the second floor, the noise wouldn't matter.

If she waited, he might find her.

Her hands trembled as she straddled the seat, keyed the ignition, and heeled the kick stand back.

No time for the niceties like helmet and jacket.

And Peter had no time left at all.

Don't wait.

She started the engine, gunned it once, and Wade Modeen stepped into the doorway.

Grinning.

Someone's coming," Jim said, figuring if it got any hotter in here, he'd melt.

Rachel uncurled from the sofa, gun in hand.

Damn, he thought as Nola's car swung off the road onto the driveway. He made to stand, but the gun waved him down. Rachel's expression was impassive, her movement almost listless as she walked into the hall and paused by the door.

"Don't hurt her."

It wasn't a plea.

Rachel smiled.

He sat up and rubbed his hands roughly over his face, trying to spark energy, trying to think of some way to get her before she got Nola.

The doorbell rang.

He rose awkwardly, legs not giving him much support, ignoring the threat of the barrel quickly aimed at his chest. His look told her he had to answer, Nola had seen his car outside, and no response would only bring more trouble.

Rachel backed away.

The doorbell rang again.

"Well, it's about time," Nola said when he answered. She pushed past him, straight into the living room, before he could stop her. "What've you been doing all day, Jimmy? Christ, it's hot in here! That damn conditioner break down again?"

She turned about in the center of the floor, just as Rachel stepped around the corner, one hand behind her, the other taking Jim's arm and pushing him ahead of her before he could react.

"Jimmy, I've been thinking about what happened last night."

He shook his head. He had no idea what she was talking about, but he wanted her out of here. Quickly.

"Nola, honey, that was last night. I've got a ton of stuff to do, and—"

"It's about them," she insisted, not sure who to look at, faint confusion gathering in a faint frown across her brow. "I tried to tell Maurice, but he had some God business to do and didn't listen."

"Nola," he said sternly, and reached for her arm.

"Jimmy, damnit." She took a step back, jutting her chin toward the other woman. "You haven't time for fooling around, you hear me? Ruby's kin, they're going to be here any minute, and there's something I got to tell you." She flashed a smile at Rachel. "Honey, you mind fetching me a glass of water? It's hotter'n an oven in here. My throat feels packed to the gills with sand."

"Be glad to," Rachel said brightly, and left.

"Jimmy," the waitress said when they were alone, lowering her voice, not taking her gaze from the hall, "I had a visitor last night."

He closed the gap between them and grabbed her arms. "Get out," he whispered. "Don't say a word, just get the hell out of here." But when he tried to push her toward the door, she resisted. "Nola!"

"Don't you 'Nola' me," she snapped. "We got trouble, and I'm not leaving until you hear me."

"I can hear you," he answered, barely moving his lips. "But I'm telling you to get out, damnit."

She glared.

He grabbed her upper arm, squeezing until she winced. "Damnit, Nola, get out, she's one of them."

He was surprised when she didn't argue, didn't question, but moved smartly to the hall. "Don't bother with that, honey," she called as she opened the door. "Jimmy's being a pain in the ass, I'll call him later."

"No," Rachel said, sliding out of the kitchen.

Little girl," Wade said, "ain't that hog a bit big for a tiny thing like you?"

Rumbling filled the garage.

Exhaust filled the hot air.

Even squinting against the glare, she could barely make him out, standing with the sun behind him, a shadowman with his hands propped mockingly on his hips.

I'm not going to die.

"Little thing, your brother's calling."

I'm not going to die.

He looked around slowly. "You want to get off that thing now? Ruthann's waiting, and she's got a temper you wouldn't believe."

She wiped her hand nervously over her hip, and he laughed, laughed again when she gripped the handlebars and gunned the engine once again.

"Now, come on, don't be doing something stupid," he told her, almost whining as his hands slipped to his sides. "That thing won't go fast enough to get by me anyway, you know that, so just shut it down, little girl. Shut it down before you get yourself hurt."

He laughed without a sound.

She picked her feet up and let the tires squeal and smoke, let the bike head for the drive, just to Wade's left.

He snarled and reached out.

She lashed out with the knife and slashed the blade across his eyes.

His scream.

The engine's roar.

Her own scream, Peter's name, as the tires spun grit and dust from the blacktop, seeking purchase, finding it, nearly losing it again as she veered left onto Potar Road and let out the throttle, hot wind in her eyes, the knife still in her hand.

She didn't look back.

She didn't celebrate.

She hadn't time.

If the others had heard, if the others knew, they would know where she was going, and they would follow or not, it didn't matter now because she would get there first. But she couldn't help the growing feeling they had somehow, magically, appeared right on her tail, an inch behind, no more, laughing, always laughing. Reaching out to take her.

When she reached the first of the Snake's sharp curves, the feeling became a rope that tugged at her, demanded, until she couldn't help it.

She looked back.

The road was empty.

Looked ahead.

Just as the bike swerved into the other lane.

Screaming again, this time at herself, while she fought the bike's momentum, wrestling it away from the far shoulder, hot wind in her eyes, the knife still in her hand,

feeling everything slow abruptly when she finally lost
control.

It was the sound of Rachel's voice more than the com-
mand that stopped them both.

Nola turned around on the threshold, one hand still on
the door, while Jim, without thinking, took a step toward
her.

Rachel didn't speak again.

She only pulled the trigger.

Too much noise; too much movement.

Jim threw an arm over his face and staggered back, expecting another shot that would take him as well. But there was only the mind-echo of the explosion, and Nola's startled cry as she fell back against the jamb.

He saw her face: *why didn't you stop her?*

He couldn't move fast enough to catch her before she slid sitting into the corner, legs outstretched, one hand up as if she could grab the wall and stand, the other limp and pale up on the floor beside her. Her skirt had skidded high over her knees. Her chest rose and fell rapidly, the front of her uniform absorbing the blood, when he scrambled to her, knelt beside her, and saw the look again.

why didn't you stop her?

Her lips moved soundlessly, neck muscles taut and corded, a wisp of hair hanging over her left eye.

He fumbled with the buttons, fingers numb, then slick with blood, and he didn't say a word, not to her, not to Rachel. He only wanted to get at the wound, staunch the bleeding. One thing at a time. He would take care of the jackal later, the hell with the rest of the Modeens. They wouldn't go away. And if they did, they'd be back.

"Jimmy." Barely heard; bubbling.

He didn't look.

The buttons wouldn't come undone.

"Jimmy."

The fucking buttons wouldn't come undone.

Her hand slipped away from the wall, and flopped into her lap.

He felt it, he didn't see it, but he rocked back on his heels and stared at the woman who had probably been his best friend. Her eyes were closed. As he watched, her head slowly sagged forward until her chin rested against her chest. His hand drifted gently to the top of her head, rested there, stroked it once, stroked it again, and pivoted around to let Rachel know.

She was gone.

Slowly, to keep his legs from cramping, he rose; slowly, to keep his balance, he took a step forward. The light was dim, almost fuzzy, motes like gnats darting across his vision as he made his way toward the kitchen. Gun or no gun, he wouldn't let her stop him until he'd taken the life from her. His fingers flexed. No weapons but his own hands. His lower lip trembled until he sucked it between his teeth and bit down, not enough to draw blood, just enough to spark pain.

He listened, but couldn't hear her.

He only heard the gun's retort, lingering with the stench of cordite in the hall.

Somewhere outside, he could hear the roar of a distant engine; somewhere inside, he thought he heard the rasp of her breathing as she tried to control it, be silent, wait for him to come to her.

All the hall doors were open.

She wasn't in his room, nor was she in the bathroom. It only took a glance; neither room was very large.

The engine, louder.

He drifted toward the righthand wall, one hand skimming the surface, while he let the kitchen move step by step into view. The counters top and bottom, the floor, the back window, the corner of the table, before he stopped, lifted his head and tried to take a decent breath in the miserable too-hot air. The only good thing, he decided, was that it made her slower as well, although he couldn't begin to imagine if that would be slow enough.

One more step would put him in the doorway.

He glanced back at the living room, thinking maybe he should have picked something from the pile she'd left in the corner; anything, it didn't matter. But his fingers flexed, and he changed his mind, and before he could change it again, he stepped quickly into the room, ready to move, ready to duck.

It was empty.

Shit, he thought, and whirled, thinking she'd ducked into the spare room, standing there now with the gun aimed at his back.

"Shit," he said aloud.

That room was empty too.

Then he realized that the back door wasn't closed all the way, just enough to prevent it from swinging open and alert him. Immediately he shoved himself against the wall, realizing how big a target he was, standing there like an idiot while she was out there somewhere, waiting for him to make up his mind what the hell he'd do now. And almost as quickly as he'd moved, he let himself relax. She wouldn't do anything. Not with the gun. He knew her better than she thought he did.

A shake of his head, both to clear it and in scolding, and he hurried up the hall, flicking on the air conditioner as he swung into the living room, averting his eyes from Nola's body. He pawed through the junk Rachel had brought in from the kitchen and bedroom until he found a small cleaver with indentations in the handle. Then he plugged the phone back in and dialed Maurice's number.

No one answered.

He started to dial Peter's when he heard the engine again, recognized it, and ran to the window.

Jonelle's bike flew over the crest of the hill, wobbling, slowing sharply, its rear tire slamming into the fence post as she tried to avoid Nola's car parked aslant behind his own. She clipped the rear fender. He was at the door when she pinwheeled onto the lawn, on the porch when she sat up and backed away groggily on her rump from the fallen silent machine.

When she realized he was there, she looked up, and he saw the blood, the scratches, the rips and holes in her jeans and T-shirt. Still holding the cleaver, he vaulted the railing and ran over, just as she tried to stand and failed. This wasn't from the spill just taken; he'd seen her take worse and walk away with little more than a couple of bruises and severely dented pride.

Something . . .

"Damn," she spat, angry tears smudging the grime spread across her cheeks. "Jim, they've—"

She saw the cleaver.

She stared at him, at the house.

His free hand took hers and pulled her carefully to her feet. "I know."

She grimaced, pulled her lips back, closed her eyes. "Took the Snake wrong," she explained wearily, limping to the stairs beside him, letting him help her up, freezing when she saw the white figure sitting motionless near the door. "Oh," was all she said.

"Rachel," he told her, no inflection at all.

"Who, that woman? The one you—"

"She's one of them."

Once inside, she knelt beside Nola, holding a lifeless hand. She looked up. "They got Peter."

Maurice did his best not to commend the officious state trooper to a lifetime of living night-duty Hell, but nothing he had said or done, truth or lie, had convinced the man not to write him the ticket, not to make him get out of the car while the cop searched it, not to give him a condescending lecture along the lines of "You're a preacher, you ought to be setting a better example."

What was worse, the cruiser had followed him, clocking him, keeping him to the legal 65, while half the damn state and all the tourists blasted past him on the two-lane highway. At one point he almost pulled over again, ready to teach the boy a lesson in respect and Christian charity, but when he checked the rearview mirror, the sneaky son of a bitch had gone.

That galled him, but it didn't prevent him from swinging the old boat up to 75 again, not slowing until he was within spitting distance of the off-ramp leading to the overpass and Potar Road. On this side there was nothing but low hills and fields dotted with grazing cattle, the road winding off to nowhere; Ryman's station was on the other, and he stopped after he'd reached the top, and stared across the road.

No movement.

None at all.

He watched as a minivan took the ramp on the other side, came to a rolling halt at the stop sign, then angled across Potar Road toward the station's entrance. It swerved suddenly, stopped in the middle of the road for a few seconds, then returned to the highway on the short service road. It took a bit of squinting and shading his eyes, but Maurice finally saw the sagging chain pulled across the entrance, one end tied around the sign's post, the other looped around a rusty barrel.

He sat back.

He licked his lips and tasted salt.

He put the engine in gear and drove slowly over the bridge, wishing hard his Lincoln wasn't so damn big. So damn *there*.

As he drifted by the station, he didn't turn his head, but saw enough—the "Closed" sign and the chain—to know Peter and Jonelle were in serious trouble. The boy may be a little on the scattered side, too sinfully attracted to the sinfully attractive ladies, but as long as Maurice had known him, he had never wasted a second when it came to making money.

Closing the station in the middle of the day was absolutely out of the question.

He passed the house.

He adjusted his outside mirror, and saw an unfamiliar car parked behind the store.

No movement.

None at all.

When he checked the house the same way, and saw the open garage, he was tempted to turn around. It wouldn't be unusual, the preacher come to call, and it would give him a chance to see who was in there, because whoever it was, it wasn't the Ryman kids.

When he realized he had eased his foot off the accelerator, however, he pressed it down again and stared so hard at the blacktop ahead, his eyes began to water until he forced himself to blink. No sense in it, he told his hands bloodlessly gripping the steering wheel; no sense in it, stopping. Doing the Lord's work was one thing; committing sure suicide was something else.

What he had to do was get to James, talk to him and that child and see if they knew where Peter had gone. What had happened to Jonelle. It might be nothing more than one of them taking sick, one taking the other to the clinic. It might be nothing more than that.

He didn't believe it.

Not for a second.

Despite the heat, he felt a chill, and while he refused to put stock in anything like premonition, he couldn't help the feeling he had finally reached the end of a long, unlit road, the one he had taken with James many years ago, the one he was positive had no church or angels waiting for him at the end. It was a foolish notion. As he took the Snake at a speed slower than a man trotting, he knew it was foolish, just his imagination working to fill the curious gaps the empty house and station had left in the natural order of things.

Nevertheless, he switched on the radio, found his gospel station, and did his best to sing along, as loudly as he could, until he topped the rise and saw the vehicles in James' driveway, and the battered motorcycle on its side, half on the grass.

He drove past the gap and parked on the shoulder.

When he stepped out, he was struck by the intensity the heat seemed to have gained even though the sun was already on its way down.

And by the silence.

There were no birds, no distant sounds of cattle or horses, no muffled sounds of traffic.

Not even a breeze husking through the weeds and leaves.

He didn't move.

He didn't move, but his eyes did, searching the house for signs of life, searching the field for signs of movement.

Something was out there.

He couldn't see it, but he could feel it.

This time it wasn't his imagination.

Something was out there, in the distant trees, behind a low knoll, crouching in the weeds, ducked behind a shrub.

James stood in the doorway.

But something was out there.

hy the hell, Jim asked, don't you hit something, or cry, or kick the walls in? Something. Anything.

Why the hell don't you scream?

But he felt nothing, and it was beginning to unnerve him.

He stood in the doorway, watching the white-suit preacher test the air as if he were a hound, and he felt nothing; he looked over his shoulder and saw Jonelle on the couch, hands draped listlessly between her knees, hair in tangles over her face, and he felt nothing.

With the first step Maurice took away from his car, he flung the cleaver down the hall, its clatter dull and flat. He tried to work the rage again as the tall man approached him, but when it stirred, he knew it was there because it was supposed to be, because he expected it, not because he really felt it.

And as Maurice wept over Nola's body, and wept again for Peter, he felt himself turn away and head for the back door, kicking the cleaver aside, stepping onto the stoop, down to the grass.

She was out there.

They were out there.

Gumdrop hills and pastures almost lush, wild flowers and weeds, the stuff of country songs and country poets and twilight mist with stars around an overhead moon.

She was out there.

Something small and dark on the lawn midway toward

the back drew him closer, paying no attention to the possible danger, that one of them might be waiting in the trees to get him alone. He didn't think so; he didn't know why. But he did know why Rachel had left his gun behind. He swiped it off the grass and tucked it into his belt, not bothering to check it.

She had used it on Nola because she had it.

She dropped it because, out here, she didn't need it.

He stared blindly at his land, at the hills he'd like to own just to keep other builders away, and nothing he could do, not a memory he could summon, was able to prod him into grieving, into shedding a single tear.

It more than unnerved him.

It scared him to death.

But before he could make at least some sort of token, private gesture, a hand grazed his shoulder, a shadow merged with his.

"You never met my Daddy," Maurice said, his voice a deep-note hymn. "Cussed a blue streak and went to church every Sunday. Got so he cussed even in his prayers. Died a happy man, I think. Last time I saw him, he was smiling anyway."

"Maurice, what the hell are you talking about?"

The preacher gestured toward the low hills and pastures dead ahead, and to the mountains climbing at them to the north. "Most of this state is like that out there. I would like to suggest that we don't try to find them unless you have some special radar hidden in a closet." The hand squeezed once and fell away. "Wasn't your fault, James. You and the Lord know it would have happened sooner or later."

"In Dunn's," Jim said, "I saw them, looked right at them, and didn't know who they were."

Maurice leaned over, plucked some grass, tossed the blades into the air. No breeze caught them; they fluttered weakly to the ground. Several fell on the toe of a badly scuffed white boot, and he realized with a slow blink that Jonelle had joined them, looking so much like a waif that he came damn close to smiling.

Maurice nodded, cleared his throat. "The Lord didn't make them like us, James, you know that. But those folks aren't like those wolf things you see on the screen."

"Werewolves," Jonelle said.

"Right, child. Werewolves."

Jim's hands found their way into his pockets, and he looked over the woman's head, seeing nothing. "The point, okay? What's the point?"

But he knew what it was; he just resented their having to make the effort to remind him. He knew there were no special-effects alterations of their bodies at night; he knew that except for those white-glow eyes, there was no concrete, photographic way he could point to one and accuse.

It was an instinct that made people nervous around them, some sixth sense that had no name in any book.

It was that same instinct that had kept him alive all these years; and the instinct that had failed him with Rachel and her brothers.

For the first time.

For the first time since that old cop had taken him on the night tour and he had learned what he had to do to avenge his sister's life, he had failed.

"James."

There had been times, a few, when he had been unable to catch one, or had been lured away by false trails, or had nearly fallen into a simple trap or ambush. But that, he figured, was to be expected. It was part of the hunt. Perfection belonged only to Maurice's God.

This wasn't the same.

This was a complete breakdown of the core of his system.

It was, in a way, the destruction of him as a Hunter.

The enormity of it, and the terror, turned him around to face the house. For a few moments he couldn't breathe; for a few moments longer he could barely see.

Jonelle took his hand. "There are things we have to do while the sun's still up." A gentle tug. He looked down, into red-rimmed eyes he had never realized before were the color of a summer night. "We have to go."

They took Maurice's car back to the station, and spent an hour searching for Peter Ryman's body.

Maurice found it in the garage, rolled under his blocked car. It was naked, its back flayed in ridges as if by claws, and half his thighs were missing. There was hardly any blood. He and Jim used a portion of tarp they found tucked up in the rafters, rolled Peter in it, and placed him in the trunk. Jonelle stayed outside; Jim didn't blame her.

They buried their friends in the field's soft loam, he and Maurice bare-chested and drenched with sweat as they dug with shovels Jonelle had taken from her garage. They spelled each other, the three of them, for nearly three hours. Saying nothing beyond an occasional grunt when they hit a rock, a curse when the digging stung. After the first few times a car passed along the road, they didn't look up, but Jonelle reloaded the gun and kept it close to hand.

The clouds moved in, taking the edge off the heat. But though they were dark and low, bringing twilight early, there was no distinctive scent of rain, no movement in the air. Sheet lightning flared once in a while over the mountains, weak, without a sound.

When they finished, the bodies wrapped in sheets and lowered, while Jim and Jonelle shoveled the dirt back in, Maurice put his suit jacket on and said a few prayers, his face unmoving though moisture glittered in his eyes.

And through it all, Jim felt nothing.

It made his hands shake.

It also shortened his temper when he noticed the others watching him, not directly, just a glance now and then, as if he was ready to explode any second and they didn't want to be around when it happened, or they were afraid they wouldn't be when it did. He held his silence, however, and when the graves were filled, and the sky below the clouds filled with swarms of birds in tattered dark ribbons heading for their roosts, he suggested they clean up, get clean clothes, and head to Dunn's bar.

"Why?" Jonelle asked, looking to Maurice, who only shrugged.

"People."

"What?"

"For the time being, I think it'd be a good idea to have some people around. It's Friday, right? God, I don't remember. The place will be packed."

"Ah." Maurice grinned. "Safety in numbers, James."

He nodded. "Right. It'll give us a chance to work out what we're going to do next."

Jonelle was still puzzled. "But I thought we were going after them."

He checked the sky; the birds had gone save for a few wandering stragglers. "We don't have to."

Ruthann paced the length of the concrete-floor cellar, feeling caged and hating it, while Bobby did his best to bind the wounds over Wade's swollen eyes.

She had heard the others return, but she hadn't worried then, and she wasn't worried now.

All they'd wanted was the boy's body.

She peered through the high narrow window opposite the stairs, and smiled for the first time since fleeing down here.

"Getting dark," she said.

Wade moaned.

"Hush," she said. "You're not going to die."

"Ruthann," Bobby said, caution in his tone.

She didn't answer.

It was getting dark.

There were so many places to hide and observe, it was laughable, and she couldn't imagine now why Momma had been so upset by this man, and why she herself had feared him. He took no special precautions against her return, not when he was alone, not when the others arrived. And when he was outside, he moved as if he had been pumped with drugs. A zombie. Or a man who knew he was already dead.

That puzzled her.

He was powerful, no question about it; at least Momma had been right about that much.

But it hadn't taken much to let his air out, just the killing of a woman. Which, for her, had been not quite distasteful, but certainly unsatisfying. Necessary, however. The bitch would have ruined everything, and she had no idea why Jim had taken her into his clan. It sure wasn't her beauty, or, she thought with a giggle, her monogamy.

Not that she cared.

After all, he was only human, and she had long ago given up trying to figure them out.

She had intended to move on once the trio had driven away in the black man's car, but curiosity held her because they hadn't taken any weapons that she could see or sense. She took some of the time until their return to hunt down a squirrel to keep her stomach from growling, spent the rest dozing in the shade, until their voices woke her.

As far away as she was, she couldn't hear the words, but she gathered from the reactions that the little girl's brother had somehow been killed. No; not somehow. Little Sister was here. She was as sure of that as the fact that the clouds, this time, threatened no rain.

As sure as she was that Jim Scott and his friends couldn't be separated now with a miracle.

Which meant she and Ruthann would have to have a little talk.

She hadn't wanted to, before. But now she realized she had underestimated the bitch. Ruthann was clever. Let Momma and Rachel do the fighting, then come in and stitch the pieces.

Clever.

Rachel snarled.

I think," Jim said, exaggerating a grimace, "my eardrums are going to burst."

As he had predicted, Dunn's Place, even this early, was crowded. They sat in the middle booth on the lefthand wall, Jim facing the door; all the other booths, and tables, and seat-back barstools were taken. In back, a huge new jukebox blared a bluegrass song, and on the new hardwood dance floor, two couples were attempting a clumsy Texas two-step. Three ceiling fans did their work, but it wasn't enough to clear the smoke from the air, or overcome the fact that the air conditioning was just weak enough to make its presence known, and not much more.

Dunn handled most of the food orders himself, grumbling about Nola's taking off like she had, accusing without words Jim and the others of covering for her again, while she was out there somewhere, having fun. For one brief period, he had Dorry in to help, but the girl was too overwhelmed by the drastic difference in clientele and had left close to tears.

Maurice's long fingers curled as he gestured to the room. "My work has so far to go when I see a place like this."

"Don't preach," Jim warned, clearing the last of his french fries from his plate.

Jonelle giggled.

"A true minister doesn't stop with a sermon in his church."

Jim showed him a mock fist. "No, but he can't do too good without any teeth."

"He will provide," Maurice answered, unfazed.

Jonelle, long used to the way the two men talked to each other, stared at her plate. The burger, evidently cooked in the same grease as the fries, was less than half finished. Jim had urged her to eat something, force herself if she had to since she'd barely had a bite all day, but she couldn't bring herself to do it. It wasn't the food; she'd eaten here many times. It was Peter. It wasn't fair to him, it wasn't fair to her that the grieving would have to wait until some vague moment in the future. She missed him already. He frustrated her, he exasperated her no end, sometimes he even disgusted her.

But Jesus, she missed him.

And felt the tears form.

Felt a hand cover hers, looked up, and saw Jim reaching across the small scarred table.

He didn't say anything.

The look was all she needed.

Bluegrass to pop country, and the two couples were joined by two others. Customers left, others replaced them. Cider had calmed down. The rake-thin bartender was joined by a long-haired woman in a tight white shirt with glittering sequins in patterns, and the neon in the window seemed brighter, and sharp-edged.

Voices rose, songs were sung.

A near fight was avoided when Cider used his ample stomach to bump the antagonists apart.

They told their stories, then, Jim taking the longest, and when they were finished, he ordered a round of beers and asked if they had any suggestions.

Jonelle said nothing, not at first. She still felt uneasy at the way he behaved when Maurice wasn't teasing him. It wasn't like him. He was the one with the ideas, not them.

He was the one leading the crusade, not them. He was the one who had so much confidence in the rightness of what he was doing that he often made her feel so much smaller than she was.

But something had happened in that house, something he hadn't told them, and she couldn't for the life of her figure out what it was.

Maurice pushed back into the corner of the booth with a groan and suggested, one hand drifting lazily over the table, that the first thing they should consider was going back to his house, not Jim's. The reason was simple—it's where the armory is. It's more solid, it can more easily be defended, it has more room to maneuver, it—

"Damn, Maurice," she said, grabbing the hand to stop its weaving. "You'd think we're up against an army. There's only three."

"Rachel," Jim reminded her.

"The gathering," the preacher reminded them both.

At that she shook her head emphatically before Jim could speak again. "After what I did . . . after all this, I don't think they're going to go looking for help outside the pack." A one-shoulder modest shrug when Jim smiled at her. "I mean, there's other kin—aunts, uncles, cousins, who the hell knows how many—but I don't think they've been told either."

Maurice questioned her with a frown.

She kept her gaze on Jim and raised a forefinger. "Ruby's dead." He didn't react; she added a second finger. "We did it." Still nothing; she added a third. "What's left is between Rachel and . . . her sister."

"Ruthann," the preacher murmured.

"Whatever. But they . . ." She stopped. She glanced at each of the men in turn, and almost didn't say the rest.

Almost. "In something like this, they take care of their own."

And when they do, what then?

They go on to something else.

"Yeah," said Jim quietly, staring at the dark, paneled wall at his shoulder.

Well, I'll be, she thought, and this time it was her hand that reached out to cover his.

"If y'all wish," Maurice said after altogether too much time had passed, and neither of them had moved, "I could probably pronounce you man and wife right here, you could go hunting on your honeymoon."

She caught him with a quick stabbing elbow, and he grunted a laugh. But it didn't stop the blush she felt working at her cheeks. *Damn you,* her look said; *mind your own damn business.*

"And what are you?" she said aloud. "The chaperone?"

His fingertips fluttered to his chest. "Me? Why, child, I'm just a humble preacher, spreading the Lord's Word, and His Wrath where necessary."

She couldn't hold the scowl. "Nola was right. You're a scoundrel."

Maurice looked at Jim. "I never did believe in college for women. It gives them an unfair press on the advantage they already have."

Then he excused himself to the men's room, and when Jonelle had slid back in to take his place, she leaned over and said, "Why is he with you?"

Jim didn't answer right away.

"I mean, he's a minister. I never did get it, and he's never said a word."

"My hair," he said.

"What?"

He pointed to the color. "It matches his suits."

Her mouth opened, closed, and when he grinned, she pinched his wrist hard enough to make him yelp.

"Okay, okay."

"Tell me."

"They took one of his angels."

The way her eyes shifted away told him she didn't require elaboration. That was all right with him. He had never, in fact, asked for or demanded full, soul-baring explanations why the folks who joined him did. As long as they did the work, knew their place, he was only grateful for the help.

Now they were down to three, and in the midst of a twinge of guilt, he wasn't sure how much he really could count on Jonelle when push came to shove. Not that he didn't trust her. Hell, from the first moment Peter had introduced them, and she had sized him up so candidly it had made him damn near shy, trust hadn't been a question. What was, however, was her handling of weapons. During normal hunts, all of them together, Jonelle was the bait, a position that had evolved, he'd once thought, quite naturally.

Now he knew it had been her idea from the start.

And she definitely knew how to use her knives.

But this time the bait would be useless.

This time, Jonelle would have to be part of the stalking, and the kill.

Maurice returned, making such a show of switching his beer mug with hers that the seriousness of her expression dissolved into delightful, helpless laughter. He couldn't join them, but he did his best not to sour the mood.

Instead, he grumbled about the music, the volume, the increasing size and boisterousness of the crowd.

They knew what he was doing, and were ready when he dropped a few bills onto the table, and said, "It's time to go."

In the parking lot, at Maurice's car, Cider Dunn waited, tossing away a cigarette as they approached.

Jim braced himself.

Dunn pointed a blunt finger at him, ignoring the others. "If you done something to chase that lady away, Scott, I'll have your hide over my bar."

Jim shook his head.

Dunn's scowl brought his eyebrows together and he stomped away over the gravel, turned at the door, and called, "Bring her back, y'hear? Don't care how, just bring her back. Damn place'll go to hell without her."

"Well, well," Jonelle said as Maurice backed onto the road.

Jim was surprised too.

But then everything these past few days seemed deliberately calculated to surprise him, bewilder him, and thrust him off balance. He didn't like it. He didn't much like surprises at all.

They all sat in front, Jonelle in the middle, the windows rolled down, the air still warm, still muggy.

Jim braced his elbow on the car, his hand cupping the roofline. "It's simple—do we wait for them to come to us, or do we go to them?"

"Look at the sky, James, look at the time. It's their

world now. As I said before, it would be foolish for us to do the moving around."

"If we hole up, it could take days."

"It will give us time to make amends for our sins."

"It'll give them time to hunt someone else. *We* can run to the store if we get hungry enough."

"It'll drive us all nuts if we stay inside," Jonelle said, matter-of-factly. "They won't have to do a thing. We'll just kill each other."

The car was parked in back, facing out.

While Jim opened the hidden closet and gave Jonelle her pick of weapons, Maurice strolled through the house. Turning on all the lights.

"I don't like guns," she said, standing uneasily in the open doorway, looking out at the barn fading by shades into the dark. She had a 9mm handgun, light enough for her size, Jim told her, but as deadly as anything else when she hit what she aimed at.

He stood behind her, frowning slightly, more aware of her now than he had ever been. It was strange. For all that he knew that she was indeed a woman, college educated, traveled, a little crusty at times, there were moments, like now, when what he wanted most was to perch her on his lap, give her a squeeze, and tell her everything would be all right. A child. A damnable thought. Insulting as all hell.

"I'll be okay, you know," she said, not turning around.

Damned mind reader, too.

He put a hand on her shoulder. "Look, I'm . . ."

Her right hand came up and held on to his.

"I'm sorry about Peter. You don't know how sorry."

"He . . . thanks." He felt a tremor; it passed. "Me, too. About Nola."

He nodded. "It may sound dumb, but she knew what she was getting into. That . . . it doesn't make it any better, but she knew the price."

"So did Peter."

"No." Her hand slipped away, tucked into her pocket. "No, sometimes I don't think he really did."

She turned, looked up, not quite frowning. Then a brief smile: "My neck's going to break."

They sat on the top step.

The air began to move.

"What I meant was, he, and you, were hardly ever part of the finding. He cleaned up. The cars go away, the . . . bodies go away. He was rear guard."

"Yes. I know that."

He tapped his temple lightly. "He knew here what they were." He tapped his chest. "He didn't really know here."

"And what's the difference?"

"Between hunting and murder."

Are we going to die?"

"You're a little young to be thinking that."

"Jesus, I'm almost thirty-one. Next December, for God's sake. What does that make you, Methuselah?"

"Sometimes, yeah."

"You didn't answer my question."

"Well, some psychologists, they'd say I died a long time ago. In a manner of speaking."

"Well, in a manner of speaking, that's a crock of shit."

"Damn, Jonelle Ryman, you know, there are times when I kind of like you."

"Yeah, well, I kind of like you too, but don't let it go to your head."

"You still want me to answer the question?"

"No."

Maurice Lion stood in his bathroom, naked, watching his reflection weep, not making a sound.

Rachel stood in the center of the clearing. She was tired of running, but she didn't want to go to that house above the gas station. Too many turns, too many corners, too many ways to be blocked, to be trapped. She didn't know how Ruthann would take seeing her again after so long, and after what had happened; Wade and Bobby didn't matter. So it was important they meet, and meet on neutral ground. If there was agreement, fine; a truce, fine; a fight, then she'd have plenty of directions in which to run. Not for long, though. Momma knew the difference between flight and retreat; so did she. One way or another, before the next dawn, she would be alone. She would be the pack. She would be what Momma could only dream about being. She would go to the gathering and take the place meant for her.

Rachel, honey, you know what pride is?

Momma, damnit, stay the hell dead.

You know what pride goeth before?

Yes, Momma, yes. Pride goeth before a fall.

No, honey, pride goeth before destruction.

Go to hell, Momma. Go to hell.

She braced her legs, raised her face to the absent moon, and after a couple of false starts, began to call her family home.

Maurice opened both doors and stood on the threshold. They were on the porch, on the top step, facing each other, backs each against a porch pillar. He looked from one to the other and wondered what had gone on while he'd been dressing. Whatever it was, James still looked lost.

He cleared his throat and they looked at him. He wore a fresh white suit and shirt, white shoes, no socks, and a fine silver chain with a silver cross around his neck. In his left hand he held a Panama hat, in his right hand a loaded shotgun.

"The Lord," he said, "may well wonder why two of His devoted children are sitting all alone out here, in clear view of Satan's kindred, just asking to be taken." He put on the hat and put the shotgun down, propping it against the wall. "But I have prayed, James, and I believe I may have a suitable answer to our problem."

James looked at him expectantly, hands lightly clasped around his up-raised knees.

"There is no reason, despite your contrary opinion, why we cannot proceed as we always do. They will know it's a trap. We may not even have to hide it. Or do it in such a clumsy manner that they will laugh at us even as they prepare to kill us. They will, through our skills, believe us desperate, frightened, willing to sacrifice ourselves if only we might have an opportunity to inflict damage upon them. We are no Samsons, James, but we can be Joshua."

"Meaning what?" Jonelle asked.

Maurice gave her a paternal smile. "Meaning, child, we may be smaller than some, and slower than some, but our faith will make us greater than them all."

It didn't surprise him that James only looked away after a polite few seconds of false consideration; he was dismayed, however, when Jonelle only shook her head in a manner too filled with doubt for his comfort.

"An alternative?" he suggested.

Something reached them on the wind.

So faint, so distant, the only reason each was sure it wasn't apprehensive imagination, that it wasn't a trick of summer darkness, was the reaction of the others.

Maurice reached inside the doorway and hit a master switch that let the night take the house.

James sat up; Jonelle scrambled to her feet.

Something reached them on the wind.

More than barking, shy of baying.

High-pitched enough that on other nights, in other places, it was mistaken for something else, cousin to an owl, perhaps, or some breed of nighthawk, to be puzzled over and forgotten.

But while it was there, even that far away, pets were restless and shadows longer.

Yes," Jim whispered. He nodded sharply. "Yes."

"Yes what?" Jonelle said.

"Charlie." A hand passed over his face, over his hair, and his smile was something only a jackal had ever seen. "There is no gathering, not of all the packs. At least not here, not this year. When he called . . . when he called, he said he had heard something, and I just assumed that's what he meant." He scowled at the dark sky. "I was wrong. The Modeens are on the move, swarming. Because they knew Ruby was being challenged, and they probably guessed this time she'd lose.

"They killed him because he was a Hunter. And because they didn't want me to know until the fight was over and they were strong again."

He stood, the others joined him, and he told them that he knew exactly what they had to do.

He knew where they were, or rather, where they would be in a little while.

As for how they were going to do it, three against the night, Rachel had unwittingly told him that as well.

"How?" Jonelle asked as they hurried inside at his direction.

He couldn't tell her, not in words either would understand.

It didn't matter.

They would learn.

He would do what he did best.

Charging out of the herd.

She moved quickly along the wooded rim of the high clearing, pacing, not wanting to, not wanting them to see how agitated she was, how anxious. Through the wind-skittish leaves she could see fragmented lights winking coldly at her from the interstate, and from the gas station whose lights had snapped on automatically at dusk; in the opposite direction there was nothing but drifting black.

Not that she seriously expected them to drive.

They had done that to her once.

That had been their first mistake.

The wind nudged her, the woodland whispered to her, trees rattled their branch sticks at her like a ceremony she had once seen in the movies. Peasants warding off evil. Trying to make enough noise to frighten the spirits away. But there were too many leaves, the rattling was muted, and she may be a lot of things, but she was certainly no spirit.

She inhaled the dry warm wind deeply, almost wishing the clouds would go away and bring home the moon. Bring her some light.

She moved to the mouth of the trail road that led up here, peered into the woods, and moved back to the edge. If they were doing this deliberately, if they were trying to humble her by not responding right away to teach her her place, it wasn't working. Momma sure knew how to do it. Willum sometimes, when he had the gumption, which was seldom. Not Ruthann, however, and definitely not her brothers.

Funny how it was, she thought, casting back to the private funeral she had witnessed that afternoon; funny how they put so much stock in others and mourned them when they were gone. If a pack worked that way, it would be useless within a month, disbanded and scattered in less than a year. Protection was what it gave her, and life, and food. She had coupled as well, but nothing had come of it, and thus far she hadn't much felt the urge to do it again.

Later; maybe later.

When the pack was hers.

When they all were hers.

Like Momma had done, like every pack leader, she would keep all the daughters and all the strong males. The weak ones would die. One way or the other.

Her teeth clicked together, echoing the branches overhead.

Where the hell were they? They didn't have all night, and the Hunter most certainly wasn't sitting around that pathetic little house, waiting for her to return. He'd be arming himself, arming the two others, and this delay was going to make things more difficult than they should be. Not impossible. Never that. Just damn difficult.

Proof, as if she needed it, that Ruthann would never be anything but a mother.

Birth and nurse, that's all she was good for.

She circled the perimeter a second time, and a third, cursing the wind when it strengthened and blew hair into her eyes; she considered calling them again, but didn't want to overdo it. Once was enough. Ruthann was a child, with a child's predilection toward spiteful disobedience. Even if she had balked the first time, Rachel counted on Bobby doing what was right.

What was right was paying heed.

What was right was listening to her.

She yanked a dead twig from a stunted pine and tossed it angrily into the dark.

A check of the road below when she heard a racing engine, but it was only someone heading away from the Junction. No doubt some drunk leaving that awful bar. They had been going by in both directions for over an hour, singly, and in groups like beetle caravans. Radios loud enough to hurt her ears, laughter like the tuneless cackling of geese.

They made her sick.

She returned to the spot where her car had been pushed over, and tried to find the damage Jim Scott told her was there. She couldn't see it. Too bad. It would have been to see what she had managed to survive.

It would have added to her conviction, born years ago, that this, this night, was the natural order of things.

Suddenly she stiffened.

There was something on the wind.

She half closed her eyes, teeth clicking, and heard it, felt it again. Scattered. Behind her.

She didn't turn around until she heard the first footsteps leave the woods.

Maurice was at the wheel, humming softly to himself, the car poised and idling at the mouth of the driveway; Jonelle sat in back, shoved to the edge of her seat, arms folded on the back between the preacher and Jim.

"We could just go," she suggested for at least the dozenth time.

Jim shook his head.

"We'll be here all night."

He didn't want them riding the road alone. If the jackals had any brains left—and they certainly would if Rachel was with them, if they hadn't ambushed and killed her—they would be watching for loners heading home tonight. And a loner that suddenly vanished before reaching the highway was as good as a warning flare. But he understood her need to get on with it, get it over.

The wait was driving him crazy.

The wind didn't help. It refused to blow steadily, only in several-minute spurts, sometimes strong, sometimes hardly worth it. It nudged the car. Leaves sailed in flocks over the hood and windshield, scratching at the glass, clinging to the wipers and quivering as if they'd been caught in a snare. Once in a while it carried the faint sound of music all the way from Dunn's Place; more often than not the rush of its passing only intensified the silence.

He sniffed, rubbed his eyes.

In a way he wished the damn clouds would break. The

way it was now, the night was too dark and too much of it moved.

He rested his left hand on the shotgun braced partway over his lap. No rifles this time. There wouldn't be much precision or distance shooting required. That's why he hadn't argued when Jonelle, after thinking it over and remembering her brother, decided against the handgun.

"You sure you can use one?"

Her answer had been a look that made him wince and turn away.

Maurice hummed.

Jonelle tilted her head to bump his shoulder.

"Not much longer," he told her, not realizing he'd been whispering until she asked him to repeat it. "The early crowd's ready to break. The guys going in now, they'll be there until Cider tosses them out."

"Hang out there a lot, do you?" She whispered too.

"Observation," he answered, not looking at her but smiling.

"My ass."

He couldn't help it: "That, too."

Maurice groaned, and after some muttering to himself, changed the car's position, angling it slightly southward, flicking the headlamps on. Dust blew through the grey light, some of it sparkling.

"I miss Peter."

He reached awkwardly across his chest, fingers stretched to brush across her cheek and nose. "You always will."

"So why doesn't it hurt now?"

"It will," he said. "Believe me. It will."

She bumped his shoulder again, but this time didn't move away. It was, for the moment, oddly comforting, and as a pickup whose radio was louder than its engine flared toward them and away, he had an equally odd thought—that in the few years he had known her, he had only kissed her once that he could remember. On her twenty-ninth birthday, when she met him at the door on the night of her party with, of all things, a sprig of mistletoe in her hand.

Maurice hummed.

The wind stopped.

He looked down the road, wishing again for the moon. If it had been out, he would have been able to see the ragged outline of the Ridge. As it was, there was only his memory to impose on the night, and that made the hill far too high, far too wooded, far too treacherous for his comfort. It was much too easy to see things that weren't there, and too easy by half to exaggerate the things that were.

Maurice stopped humming.

Jim looked across him toward the Junction. "Yes," he said. "I think the wagon train's coming."

Jonelle backed away.

He missed the touch, but held the shotgun.

Three, then four pairs of headlights swept around the hill, not traveling very fast. One thumping stereo fought with another; a fifth car trailed half a minute later, trying to catch up, one of its headlamps out.

Maurice pulled smoothly in behind it, keeping close without tailgating. He started humming again.

"Oh boy," Jonelle said.

Jim deliberately refused to think more than one step ahead. He stared at the bleached trunk of the vehicle they followed, couldn't make out how many riders were inside. One step. That's all. Get to the Ridge in one piece.

His right arm stretched out, his hand gripping the dashboard as if the preacher were speeding. He pulled it back a few seconds later, and a heartbeat after that began to rub the back of his neck. When he felt what he was doing, he dropped the hand into his lap where it recoiled from the touch of the shotgun's cool barrel. The dashboard again, then a light scratching of his chest, two fingers inside his shirt.

"You don't stop it," Maurice said without turning from the road, "I'm gonna cut that thing off."

Jim looked at him quickly, looked away to stare at the road's shoulder as it blurred beside the car. Something in the man's voice. It wasn't fear, it wasn't nerves, it was damn close to misgiving. It didn't take him long to figure out it wasn't about the hunt. Which immediately made him want to reassure him, to tell him he was going to be all right. This night was different. This whole damn week had been different. In just a few short days they had broken the back of a major pack, and were about to make sure it wouldn't walk again for years. The in-fighting would be horrific, and the odds were, he'd told them earlier, the pack would finally scatter, remnants joining others who would move into the vacuum.

Nature's balance.

There were respites.

There were no endings.

So why do you do it? Jonelle had asked; *if you're never going to win, why do you do it?*

That's when he'd told them to get ready and get in the car.

"Couple of minutes," Maurice said. "The boy up front, the first one, he's slowing down. Too drunk for the Snake."

It was almost too good to be real. Had the drivers
decided this parade was too tame for Friday night, the
road would have looked and sounded like a NASCAR
rally, the center line ignored, taking even the most gentle
curves as close to the inside as they could without falling
into a ditch. Dropping out of something like that, something so noisy, would have been too obvious. This was
damn near perfect, and as long as that guy up ahead didn't
wonder what had happened and stop when his follower
suddenly vanished, something like this might almost be
called a sign.

"Coming up," Maurice said, and reached for the light
switch.

No one responded.

Jim wiped his eyes with the tips of two fingers, then
cupped them around the door's handle.

Without warning, the night went black.

T he wind kicked again, harder.

This time it carried the soft scent of rain.

M aurice yanked the car over to the left shoulder as soon
as he had turned the headlamps out, using gears and
parking brake to stop them on the grass, well off the road
in case someone else wandered along.

Before the car stopped moving, Jim was out, shotgun in his right hand, left hand out to snare Jonelle's wrist and pull her into the open. They hurried around the ticking hood and joined the preacher, who had already taken the first step on the narrow road that led up to the Ridge.

They didn't run.

The surface was rough and clear enough of debris beneath their boots that veering into the trees wouldn't be much of a problem as long as they didn't take it too fast.

A gust slapped his face.

He held on to Jonelle's hand.

Maurice took the point, sweeping the way up for depressions and fallen branches that would trip them, or wrench an ankle, break a leg. The white of his suit had turned a spectral grey. Sometimes it was there, sometimes it wasn't.

The woods found a voice, rustling and clacking softly, and the way the wind moved through it, it sounded as if it had also taken legs and was moving with them.

They can't see us, Jim thought, resisting the urge to kick aside a large stone; we can't see them.

Several minutes passed before he stopped straining his eyes to see through the black. That way lay blindness. What he had to do was see the way in daylight. Not perfectly. Just enough. Remembering that a short way ahead, the road dipped sharply and rose again, and beyond that it rose just as sharply for a good fifty yards before leveling to an easier grade as it made for the top. The anticipation was dangerous; even so, it was better than not knowing a thing.

Dampness crawled down his face.

A finger's brush across his cheek told him a mist had begun to fall.

He heard his own labored breathing and snapped his lips shut, steadying his lungs, telling himself to hang in there, there was no need to hurry. If the jackals were there when they arrived, it would be over, hard and quick; if they weren't, if he'd guessed wrong, there were other nights and other roads.

Jonelle gasped in surprise as she stumbled, and pulled her hand free.

Great, he thought sourly when the wind shifted and blew at his back. But there was nothing he could do. Either they caught his scent, or they didn't. Everything, tonight, was only one way or another. There was no third option.

Into the dip, and he nearly lost his balance, ordered himself to stop thinking, pay attention, and hurried up the other side. Maurice waited for him, took his elbow and gestured quickly—he had heard something up there.

Jim took the lead, slightly hunched over as the grade steepened and the wind pushed him harder, shifting yet again, this time from the left.

The mist clung to his face.

Strands of hair darted over his cheeks and forehead, feeling like spiders in a hurry.

A pause, left hand stretched back to keep the others from colliding with him.

He heard it.

He heard voices.

The left hand became a fist as his eyes closed tightly, tight enough for sparks, before he opened them and moved on. Maybe thirty yards more before the trees parted for the clearing. He could see brief outlines of foliage that caught the light from the gas station, and from the traffic on the highway. It wouldn't be enough for him to see clearly once he got there, but it would give him a fair sense of where the open space ended and the drop-offs began.

He stopped a third time, waited for the others, and when they reached him, they huddled, heads nearly touching as they used the wind now for cover.

"Got them?" he asked Maurice.

The preacher reached into his jacket pockets and pulled out three small flashlights just over six inches long. Though they looked like the plastic kind found in any hardware store, almost any supermarket, they were fitted with bulbs that were a good ten times brighter; but the batteries wouldn't be able to hold all the power the bulbs needed, so the intense illumination wouldn't last very long.

Long enough, he hoped, to momentarily blind who-ever stood in its way.

They clipped them to their belts.

"Left," he told Jonelle; "Right," he told Maurice.

They nodded.

The mist thickened.

The wind crept into his shirt.

Though there was no time for speeches, pep talks, final wisdom, he made a determined fist he held up and bran-dished twice. Maurice winked, and moved away. Jonelle stretched up and kissed his cheek, patted it, and moved away.

Touching the light in his left hand to be sure it aimed forward, hefting the shotgun in his right, he did his best to stay in the center of the road. It was rutted here, used by the clearing for storm run-off, and several times he found himself wobbling to his knees. There was no mud yet, but the mist had already made the surface slick.

Slow down, you idiot.

He couldn't do it.

The wind brought voices.

Lower, then, almost to his knees as the ground leveled, the wind stronger because the trees had finally fallen away.

Voices in the dark.

Two women, but he couldn't tell whether they were arguing or not.

Closer, slower, fighting to keep his breathing even.

Closer still, and impatiently he blinked the gathering moisture from his eyes, unable to tell if this was prelude to a downpour or nothing more than it was.

You've lost it, you know.

He shook his head sharply.

Couldn't tell them when they weren't even ten feet away.

The shotgun's stock slapped against his thigh.

Couldn't even tell when one of them was right in your own goddamn house.

One of the voices rose in a single word, like a bark, and he recognized it at once—Rachel. Having trouble, maybe, getting the others to work with her to get rid of the hunters, or trying to convince them she had nothing to do with Ruby's and Willum's deaths.

A point for his side: it didn't sound as if they were in the embrace of filial cooperation. Still, it would be too much to ask that Ruthann had decided she might run the pack on her own, without help from her older sister.

A stone darted out from under his right foot, and he went down hard on his knee.

The voices stopped.

The wind died.

The only sound aside from his own breathing the muffled growl of a truck below on the highway.

He waited.

He listened.

A man's voice, then, perfectly clearly: "Y'all are wasting time."

"Shut up, Bobby." Ruthann.

"Well, we ain't got all night, and they ain't sitting on the porch, rocking and smoking until we show up."

"This is stupid, I keep telling you. Why don't you listen?" Another man, uncertain and uneasy. "We should be heading on, forget this, okay? We can bring the others, they know Scott, and we won't have anything to worry about."

"Hush!"

Jim started.

It was Rachel.

Still on one knee, he reached the road's end, and saw them. Little more than stick figures, but he could see them. Rachel stood to his right, facing another woman that must be Ruthann. Two men sat on the ground, their backs to Jim. The faces were hidden, the occasional flicker of light from the road and highway less effective than decent starlight.

If he waited long enough, it was possible the women might go ahead and fight, right here, going for the throat. But he didn't think it likely. This quartet was the last of the main branch of the Modeens, and even in their mutual distrust and anger, they surely had to know what they would lose if they even lost just one.

"Listen—"

"Wade, I told you to hush!"

Wade grabbed a pebble from the ground and tossed it angrily aside. "Who the hell died and made you boss?"

"Momma," she answered flatly. "And it was Jim Scott that did it."

Jim rose to his full height.

The wind picked up, staying high, tipping the crowns of the dark trees; the mist thickened into near fog.

"Well, listen," said the other man, "I'm getting hungry, and if you two don't stop it soon, me and Wade are heading to the road."

Rachel turned on him. "You'll do as you're told, Bobby Modeen."

Jim could hear the nasty smile in his voice: "I don't think so, Rachel. Not yet I don't think so."

Stick figures shifting, still on the ground but moving behind Ruthann.

Jim allowed himself a smile of his own.

"I'll do it alone if I have to," Rachel told them.

"No, you won't," Ruthann said. "You'll be dead, just like Momma."

Stick figures shifting without leaving their places.

Jim raised the flashlight, pointing it like a gun.

And froze.

Stick figures lifting, and freezing, finally falling to all fours. A hissing from one, snarling from another, and from Rachel a low whistling just this side of a howl.

are they human?

i think so.

They didn't sound human at all.

Bracing the shotgun snugly against his side, he switched on the light, and almost immediately the other beams exploded from either side while he averted his eyes quickly to keep his vision intact.

He wanted to say something then—for Peter, for Nola, for poor damn Charlie Acres—but he couldn't say a word, and he couldn't pull the trigger.

They hadn't moved, not an inch, except to turn their heads to locate the source of the intrusion. Their faces, washed of shadow in the brilliant white, were distorted, lips snarling, teeth bared, flesh pulled back to give them the look of skulls.

And their eyes glowed dead white.

Not human at all.

He had never seen them like this, not even on the night that old cop had introduced them. Not so starkly. Not so clearly. Not so clearly inhuman. He came close to despair at yet another mistake, his left arm lowering just a fraction, because all these years he had truly believed he'd known them, but he had never known them like this.

"James," Rachel whispered-whistled softly, not frightened at all.

Slowly Jim brought the shotgun up.

Too slow.

Too damn slow.

"James."

He recognized it in the instant before the first of them moved.

The trap.

The bait.

It was too late.

The game had to be played.

Without visible signal, they flung themselves apart high and low, snarling, close to barking, as Jim fired at Rachel and missed. Fired again, while Maurice fired, Jonelle fired, their lights swinging madly to be swallowed by the low clouds, scattered by the misty fog.

Firing again as the jackals scattered for the trees, not for him or the others, and when the first blast tore the ground not five feet from where he stood, he cried out a hasty warning and fired at one who had stumbled near the perimeter between him and Jonelle.

The pellets caught his leg, and Wade went down, screaming, howling, rolling over, clutching his shin.

Lights swept the clearing erratically, moving closer toward the center.

"No!" Jim shouted when Maurice blasted a shadow, taking a branch off its trunk near where Jonelle should have been.

Lights punching through the dark, accentuating the fog.

Wade scrambled to one knee, left leg dragging.

Jim started over, chambering a round, but one of the beams caught Jonelle full in the chest as she walked out of the woods, flaring off her shirt, and the sudden glint of a blade.

He couldn't see her face.

He could see the arm, the fingers that grabbed a handful of the boy's hair, could feel the wrenching back, could see the knife slice swiftly and deeply across his throat.

But he couldn't see her face.

Maurice fired into the trees.

Jim ran to the center, turning in a careful circle, the trunks and leaves a sickly grey as the beam swept over them too fast, much too fast. Too many shadows moved

in too many directions, too many branches looked too
different, and as the preacher trotted to his side, he
switched the light off before it died on its own.

A moment later Jonelle joined him, and he put a hand
to her cheek.

Just to know she had a face.

"Like the boy said . . . stupid," Maurice muttered,
sweeping the clearing once more before extinguishing
the beam.

Jim agreed, panting to keep his adrenaline from pushing him too hard.

Amateur night is what this fiasco had turned out to be.
Goddamn amateur night, the jackals using his own fire-
power to work against him, no doubt hoping that the
hunters would kill or disable themselves while they themselves escaped without harm. It was so obvious a ploy, he
should have recognized it from the start, when they
hadn't moved at the first flash of light; hell, before it
began. They had used one of his own simple tricks against
him.

By now, with their speed, they could be halfway to
Missouri, and he was left with only one of them on the
ground. A male. Which, on any other hunt, would have
been just fine.

Christ, he thought, glaring up at the night; Christ!

T hey heard it:
  james

Maurice was afraid.

To work so long to do the Lord's will, to purge the evil, yet knowing in his heart that the ones who now prowled around the top of the ridge were still, at the core, decidedly, if evilly, human.

And to be so wrong.

Fog drew a damp shroud over his face.

Lord, I have seen them.

He couldn't keep his finger from dancing off the trigger, dancing back; he couldn't find the nerve to turn the flashlight back on.

If he did, he might see them.

The eyes were bad enough, hellish without the hellfire, but the distortions he had seen in what had been human faces were far worse than the condition of the angel that had set him on this road.

He was going to die.

Out there now, hissing, snarling, moving in a great slow circle to keep him moving in a circle of his own, was the one who would kill him. Butcher him. Devour him.

He moaned, and James took brief and gentle hold of his arm.

He had seen the anguish in the Hunter's expression before the last light had died, the recrimination he had taken to his heart for being led to this place when he thought he'd been doing the leading. For him, then, to make the gesture put tears in Maurice's eyes.

But still, he was going to die.

The fog thickened.

Out there, invisible, one of them laughed softly.

Soon they'd be able to walk right up to him, be not six feet away before he could see them. By then it would be too late. They were fast. And quick, very quick. He would barely have time to pull the trigger once. If he missed, he wouldn't be able to pull it again.

His shoulders rolled, his legs shifted, his hands eased and tightened their grip on his weapon.

If it's to be, Lord, just don't let me scream, and don't let me leave without at least one good pop. I'd hate that. I surely would hate leaving without one of them bleed-ing.

james

She stood with her back to Jim's right side, shotgun in one hand, knife in the other. When she fired the first time, she'd nearly been knocked off her feet. Then she had seen what those things were trying to do and had taken out the blade.

It was luck that had brought that male to his knees.

It was Peter who had driven her out of cover to finish it, barely thinking at all when her blade took its blood.

She supposed she ought to be feeling something now, some kind of reaction, but it was all she could do to concentrate on the dark, hoping to see something out there before it saw her.

Right now, it was Jim she feared, and feared for.

She could tell by the feel of his faint trembling against her back that he believed more strongly now that whatever it was that had set him apart from the others, and set him apart from the jackals, was lost. Really lost.

Revenge for Maryanne had been sated long ago.

It had become something else, and until he learned what it was, he'd be no different than he had been before the hunting started.

A brief violent shudder made her turn, eyes straining, until she heard him sucking air harshly through his mouth.

"What?" she whispered.

He shook his head.

She insisted.

He shook his head.

"So now what?"

He didn't move at all.

james, pretty james

The clearing was a hundred feet across, maybe less, he figured, and right now they were close to the drop that ended at the Snake's midpoint. Mostly rock and erosion slides, with a few trees and shrubs rooted along the way. With their hands free, they might make it to the road with a minimum of injury; the jackals weren't spiders, they couldn't climb up or down walls any better than anyone else. The problem would be at the bottom—could they make it to Jonelle's house before the jackals caught them?

With a series of nudges and gestures, he told Jonelle to protect her limited vision, and got Maurice to unclip his light and sweep it in a wide semi-circle before them, then douse it.

A frantic scurrying made him smile.

They could see ten, fifteen feet before the fog formed its wall.

Too damn close, but the illusion of distance was at least a small comfort, which was more than they had before.

The wind still blew, and still stayed high. The fog wouldn't rise, but it wouldn't dissipate either.

He had seen it move instead—stray drafts curling it upon itself, thinning it in one place, turning it to smoke in another.

Jonelle's light made the circuit.

He could feel Maurice counting, and tugged at his arm to pull his ear down. "Regular will give them a clue."

The preacher nodded.

"They're not gone," Jonelle whispered, not quite a question.

He nodded. Rachel, at least, wouldn't leave. She was the one calling his name; she was the one, if she wanted to lead, who would have to kill the Hunter.

Ruthann knew it, too.

He used his foot to tap the others' ankles, raised his

shotgun, and fired blindly into the fog. He felt Maurice stiffen, felt Jonelle jump. He also felt her smile. Then he tugged again, and brought them each down on one knee.

"We'll be here all night," Jonelle said, lips nearly brushing against his ear.

"No. They won't wait that long."

Maurice agreed. "That girl," he said. "The other one. We might use her."

"Never happen," Jonelle said.

Jim aimed his light; nothing out there but the fog.

Toward the mountains he heard the wind begin to cry.

pretty james

Girl's screwing with your mind, James."

"She went to college."

Jonelle shifted. "She's trying to scare us."

"Too late," Maurice said, no music there at all.

Jim shifted to his other knee, sensing a change in the night, feeling stronger drafts push past and through him now and then. He didn't like it. If the fog left, they would have the sight, but the jackals wouldn't have the extra cover.

They were fast.

They weren't that fast.

They'd be tempted to leave.

On the other hand, the flashlights wouldn't last much longer. Once again he kicked himself for not bringing regulars with him. What was it he had thought the other day—getting older, getting slower? Right; especially in the head.

Signaling that he had to stand or grow too stiff, he rose and flexed his knees, pointed the light, and saw a shadow flash from right to left.

He fired.

Without needing instruction, Maurice and Jonelle fired as well, each just ahead of the other.

No sound; they had missed.

"Bold little bastards," Jonelle complained, reloading.

Or desperate, Jim thought; good God, suppose they're desperate?

He backed off until his heels scraped the rocky edge of the cliff. A glance down showed him nothing. He didn't dare turn on the flash because it would tell them what he was up to, although he wondered if it really mattered. They'd either take the easier slopes through the woods, or the road, or they'd try to follow. Either way, once he was down there, he sure wouldn't be able to just walk away.

Maurice turned toward him, looked over his shoulder, and closed his eyes for just a second.

He knew.

Jim lifted an eyebrow—*you got a miracle up your sleeve?*

A sudden husking rush made him straighten, step to one side with his weapon up and ready, but Maurice just as suddenly arched his back, threw up his hands, and started to fall, his mouth wide in a silent choking scream.

Jim emptied his hands to catch him.

Jonelle used her light and fired several shots in swift succession across the clearing's center.

Something shrieked out there.

She fired again.

Jim eased the big man to the ground, half on his lap, and checked his back with his light.

"Aw, Jesus."

Jonelle dropped her shotgun and reached for her hip as she darted into the fog. He called out; she didn't stop; and Maurice moaned, shook his head. "O Jesus, O Lord, Jesus H, James, O Jesus."

The suit jacket had been shredded across the spine just below the shoulder. While he couldn't see bare skin, there was blood; too much blood.

Maurice arched his back again.

"Lord, Lord, take it away, take it away."

Laughter in the dark, quiet and mocking.

"We have to go down, Maurice."

"O Jesus, take it away! No, James, I can't." He groaned and spasmed, nearly breaking free of the helpless grip.

An agonized grunt, somewhere in the clearing.

No laughter this time.

Jim searched for his shotgun and pulled it close, trying not to move Maurice as he searched and found that one as well.

"O Jesus, Lord."

His light, much dimmer and growing visibly worse, tried to show Jonelle the way.

He couldn't see her.

"Jesus."

"Maurice, we have to go."

"I can't do that, O Jesus, James, I can't, don't make me."

Jim wanted to hit him; he pushed lightly instead, trying to maneuver the man onto his knees. The preacher groaned, but he moved, and Jim didn't know whether to scream or weep when the man spasmed and nearly fell. This time, however, big hands braced themselves on the ground, head bowed, while Jim snatched up both weapons, the light still searching for Jonelle in the fog.

Maurice rocked forward suddenly, then flung himself back and up, face contorted and lifted to the sky, bloodied lips pulled away from his teeth. He jerked back a little, sideways, then found a measure of equilibrium where the pain seemed to be slightly diminished. His head was cocked left, his cheek nearly resting on his shoulder; his left hand was hooked uselessly into his jacket.

"Jonelle!"

No answer.

pretty james

"Jonelle!"

pretty james, a taunting echo.

The flashlight faded quickly.

Jim reached for Maurice's sleeve, grabbed it, and slipped away when the preacher lurched alarmingly to one side. Hissing. Head trembling. A rush of blood slipping black down the sides of his chin.

"You first," Jim snapped, moving out of the way.

Maurice didn't move.

The light nearly died.

"Go, damnit!" Not caring now, he slapped at the preacher's arm, braced himself against the low moaning scream. "Maurice, for God's sake, hurry up."

Maurice toppled forward, caught himself with his right

hand, and struggled toward the edge, a huge three-legged dog. Hissing the entire time.

"Jonelle!"

A sudden wind-slap turned his head, and he nearly moaned himself when he saw the fog shred and boil away, and felt the mist shift to rain. They'd never make it now. The rocks would be too slippery, no place for a grip.

"O Jesus, Lord," a whisper behind him.

The light no longer reached across the open ground, but it was far enough for him to see the body not fifteen feet away. It was sprawled on its back, one hand raised and frozen as though trying to claw at the night.

It had no face; it had been either blown, or cut, away.

It was Bobby Modeen.

There was no sign of Jonelle.

Laughter again, from two places in the dark.

Jackals, he thought wildly; God, they sound just like jackals.

A flare of dead white eyes.

His light went out

He retreated again, felt a fumbling hand on his hip and whirled just as Maurice thrust his own flashlight at him. He grabbed it, switched it on, and spun back again, catching Ruthann in its beam as she darted toward the road. He fired blindly from the hip, and nearly broke his wrist, reacting too fast to brace for the recoil.

She dove to the ground, rolled over, and stood.

Hands on her hips.

White eyes.

Glowing eyes.

james, from somewhere else.

A swing left showed him nothing but the quicksilver fall of light rain.

james

A swing right, trying at the same time to see where Ruthann had disappeared to, and again there was nothing but trees and the rain.

"O Jesus."

"Get moving, Maurice," he said quietly, angrily.

james pretty james

Right again, but not all the way. He checked himself in mid-sweep and spun instantly back, grinning mirthlessly when Ruthann was caught streaking toward him from a spot not twenty feet away.

He didn't think.

He fired.

She rose shrieking to her feet, fingers clawing at the top of her skull, took one stagger-step toward him before he fired again, dropped the shotgun and picked up the preacher's.

He didn't need it.

She was curled on the ground, one foot twitching, kicking weakly.

pretty james right next to his ear.

He yelled in fright as he turned, and heard Maurice yell as well, his arms up, his mouth wide, as something quick, something *fast* raced between them, not allowing him to fire in case he hit the preacher.

It didn't matter.

The white jacket changed color, the white shirt turned to ribbons, and Maurice screamed, "O Jesus!" just once before he fell.

Nothing moved.

Only the wind.

Only the rain.

He could end it now. He could follow Maurice over the edge, hoping he'd be able to keep from falling or slipping too much. Move fast, the hell with safety, and if he reached the bottom in one piece, he'd head for the gas station. He had the shotgun and plenty of ammunition stuffed into his pockets. After what had happened up here, she would be forced into caution.

And if she wasn't, he would have her.

He could end it now.

But he still didn't have Jonelle.

The rain eased; the wind didn't.

Maurice's flashlight was dying, but he kept it on anyway, making regular sweeps through the night, fainter but still effective. Every arc passing over the upraised claw of Bobby's hand.

Rachel stood at the mouth of the road.

He didn't fire, he only watched her, both of them knowing his killing range was a good deal closer.

She raised her chin a little and called over the wind, "Thank you, James. I knew you would do it."

Unthinking, he gestured a *don't mention it* with his flashlight hand, and when he found her again, she was ten feet closer, and ten feet to his right.

Something moved out there, something else, to the left.

He shifted the beam, saw nothing, and shifted it back, and she was closer still, and shaking her head.

"I'll let you climb," she called, pointing toward the drop.

"Fine. And then what?" he couldn't help calling back.

The rain returned, a little harder, diffusing the weakened beam, blurring her moving figure. His hair clung to his forehead, partly over his eyes; he used a forearm to clear them, the light wild and cut with silver.

When he steadied, she was still there, but he couldn't see her face.

He really didn't want to.

"I go away, find the family," she told him, as if he ought to have known not to ask such a stupid question.

"But you'll be back."

"Oh yes." Still moving, she nodded. "Oh yes."

She skipped into a slow trot, never looking away, keeping out of range but staying in the light as it tracked her side to side. Faster. A little faster. Wind at her back and now in her face. Faster. A little faster.

But not moving any closer.

"You need the rest," she told him, and burst into quick laughter.

He could shoot, disrupt her rhythm, and charge her before she regained what she lost. But if he failed . . .

Faster.

A little faster.

He could barely keep the beam on her, and an accurate shot now was impossible. She knew it, and he knew she was only showing off. This, she told him, was the jackal he would have to deal with for the rest of his life.

Ruby had been a fair opponent.

Rachel would be his death.

Faster.

The light dimmed.

A ghost running, spinning once and dropping to all fours.

Faster.

Much faster.

Bobby's hand still reaching, as if trying to pull the beam down.

He checked to see how much farther he could go before he fell, and nearly lost his balance. A single step would have done it. And just below the edge a wind-whipped bush he could grab to lower himself to the ledge he thought he had seen just below. It would tear his hands open. He could hear water already running down a crack.

He stopped trying to follow her, but she didn't stop running, and she didn't stop laughing, and he knew she had changed her mind.

It wouldn't do for him to survive.

In the night world of the jackals, there was no such luxury as mercy.

She faced him now, whipping through the beam as fast as he could spot her. White eyes. White teeth. Features smeared by the rain and speed. Feinting toward him, and away, and when the wind paused and there was only the rain against the leaves, he couldn't hear her moving.

james

He watched her.

james

He watched her.

james

He saw her smiling, and suddenly realized how close she was, how she'd been moving closer all the time, and all the time he'd only watched her, hypnotized, mongoose and cobra.

He held the flashlight and shotgun in one hand and raised the weapon; she laughed as he struggled to hold the weapon steady.

One shot; he was only going to get one good clear shot. After that, if he failed, he'd have to drop the light and try to kill her in the dark.

pretty james

He brought the shotgun to his shoulder, the light wobbling, his aim untrue.

pretty

Suddenly she shrieked more in anger than pain, and tumbled, slamming her head and shoulder on the rocky ground.

He didn't question, he only ran, following her as she tried to regain her feet, arms flailing, falling again, screaming again, not anger but in rage, one hand reaching desperately for her right leg while she hopped backward on one foot. Baring her teeth as he approached her, puzzled until he saw the knife buried deep in her thigh.

She snarled and whirled to run, and fell heavily on her side, crab-crawled and turned again, sitting while she grabbed the slippery handle of the blade and tried to yank it free.

She screamed and tried again.

It wasn't human.

He didn't feel a thing when he raised his shotgun and pulled the trigger.

And didn't blink when the shotgun jammed.

He only tossed it aside and walked toward her, staring at those eyes caught and glowing in a new beam, a little stronger, that flared from just behind him.

Rachel gave up trying to get the blade out from the muscle that held it, and tried to get to her feet instead, but he reached down before she could escape him, and took her wrist, yanked her up and pulled her toward him while he stepped out of the way and pulled her toward him again.

She was strong.

He was stronger.

He yanked, and she screamed and tried to slash his eyes and flail for balance with her free arm.

He yanked and pulled, she screamed and stumbled, and he yanked and pulled her one more time.

Stepped aside, and let her go.

And watched her pinned in dying light as she spun over the Ridge's edge.

Then the light went out, and she was gone, and there was nothing left but the crying wind.

onelle came up beside him, limping badly, blood on her cheek and chin. "What do we do now?"

"Maurice," he said.

"What about her?"

They would leave her and her kin to be found, for the police to make something of it if they could. Suicide, murder, he didn't give a damn.

She slipped an arm around his waist as they headed for the road. "For balance," she explained. "I think my ankle's torn." She had cut Bobby as she'd raced past him, but lost her footing as she realized one of his claws had gashed her foot. Into the woods, then, and a makeshift bandage, waiting until she could see again without fire. "I was afraid when you called."

She had done the right thing; answering would have brought one of the women on her.

At the foot of the Ridge he climbed behind the wheel of Maurice's car and used the spare keys under the seat to start the engine. Jonelle began to shiver, and stayed inside when he drove around the Snake and found Maurice on his back, staring at the rain. He put the body in the back seat, and made a quick search for Rachel.

He couldn't find her until he looked up, and saw her looking at him.

He started, closed his eyes, and opened them again to watch the blood and rain drip from her hair across her eyes. White eyes no longer glowing.

He tilted his head and saw the dead branch thrust through her stomach.

He smiled grimly as he walked away; she may have been quick, but she sure couldn't fly.

They buried Maurice beside Nola and Peter as the sun rose and the rain still fell.

He brought Jonelle to the Junction clinic, saw the concern in the doctor's face, and the blank look in hers. He waited for nearly an hour while they debated sending her on to Knoxville, and didn't like their tone when he was told she'd have to go.

"Stay here," she said as they loaded her into the ambulance.

He had one foot on the bumper, ready to climb in.

"Please," she said, and closed her eyes.

There were things to do, but he didn't want to do them. He sat in the living room and watched the clouds thin, watched the rain fall, watched traffic drift by in shades of grey. He would give Maurice's house to his angels, as long as they promised to let him in now and then; he would find a way to help Cider replace what they both knew was irreplaceable; he would tear this house down and build something a little larger, definitely more solid.

Appropriate stones for the graves of the boy and his best friends; when the right time came, and he would know when it was, he would move them so they'd be able to rest beside Charlie.

The rain stopped, and sunlight brightened.

Shortly after five the telephone rang.

A doctor in Knoxville explained that Jonelle's foot had been badly mangled, muscles and tendons torn; some repair was possible, but there'd be a long and painful period of recuperation and therapy, and even then she would walk with a bad limp for the rest of her life.

"When can she come home?"

"A few weeks. We'll see."

H e thought about the pack.

By now, he supposed they knew what had happened up there on Potar Ridge, and there would be a time of fierce in-fighting as one or another of the females sought to take Ruby's place.

By this time next year, he supposed they'd be back on the roads.

What he didn't know was what he would do about it.

The telephone rang.

"If you don't come get me next Friday," Jonelle said,

sounding a little groggy, a little pained, "I'm going to walk home, and it'll be on your head."

He propped his feet on the sill. "The doc said a few weeks."

"I convinced them otherwise," she answered, Southern belle in her accent. "These boys are just helpless, Jim, you know what I mean?"

He nodded. "I think I do."

Something in the field across the road.

"Now what?" she asked.

"I don't know," he admitted.

"I see."

He didn't think so.

"You will," she said at last.

Something large.

"What makes you so sure?"

She yawned; he laughed.

"Remember what that bitch said?"

He waited.

Something fast.

"The natural order of things, Jim. You will because it's what you do. It doesn't matter what happened." A muffled voice interrupted her, she snapped at it, and said, "They're going to make me go to sleep, Jim. I have to go."

He wished her sweet dreams, but she wouldn't hang up. Instead she argued for a few seconds with the other person in the room, then said quickly, "But don't you damn dare do it without me, you understand?"

The line went dead.

The receiver dropped onto its cradle, the phone was placed on the floor beside his chair.

It was nightfall before he smiled.

At what Jonelle said, at the memory of Maurice and his godawful sermons, at the memory of Charlie's hound, at the memory of Nola Paine.

At the low mournful whistling he heard out in the field.

He would wait, Jonelle was right; there was healing to be done.

But there would always be cars abandoned on the road, and people would always vanish without a trace, without a sign.

There would always be eyes out there, eyes that glowed moon white.

And there would always be a Hunter.

Charging out of the herd.